If she only knew...

She would definitely have second thoughts about trekking through the wilds of Montana with him for three very long days and nights. If she really had her eyes wide open she would see how badly he wanted her and what he had in mind. Because to Stone, Madison Winters was everything a woman was supposed to be.

She was more than just a prim city girl; Madison was sensuality on legs—a gorgeous pair of them—and Stone was a hot-blooded male.

Had it only been one day since he'd first looked into eyes so mesmerizing they had taken his breath away? Even now the undercurrents of tension and attraction that enveloped Stone whenever Madison was near threatened to overwhelm him.

He wanted her and he meant to have her. But no matter how hot their passion, it wouldn't change anything for him. Because Stone had made up his mind a long time ago: There was no room for a permanent woman in his life.

BRENDA JACKSON

Stone Cold Surrender

Silhouette Books

Published by Silhouette Books

America's Publisher of Contemporary Romance

SILHOUETTE BOOKS

ISBN 0-373-28551-5

STONE COLD SURRENDER

This edition published by arrangement with Harlequin Books S.A.

® and TM are trademarks of Harlequin Books S.A., used under license. Trademarks indicated with ® are registered in the United States Patent and Trademark Office, the Canadian Trade Marks Office and in other countries.

Visit Silhouette Books at www.eHarlequin.com

Printed in U.S.A.

Books by Brenda Jackson

Silhouette Desire

*Delaney's Desert Sheikh #1473
*A Little Dare #1533
*Thorn's Challenge #1552
Scandal between the Sheets #1573
*Stone Cold Surrender #1601
*Riding the Storm #1625
*Jared's Counterfeit Fiancée #1654
Strictly Confidential Atttraction #1677
Taking Care of Business #1705
*The Chase Is On #1690

*Westmoreland family titles

BRENDA JACKSON

is a die "heart" romantic who married her childhood sweetheart and still proudly wears the "going steady" ring he gave her when she was fifteen. Because she's always believed in the power of love, Brenda's stories always have happy endings. In her real-life love story, Brenda and her husband of thirty-three years live in Jacksonville, Florida, and have two sons.

A USA TODAY bestselling author, Brenda divides her time between family, writing and working in management at a major insurance company. You may write Brenda at P.O. Box 28267, Jacksonville, Florida 32226, by e-mail at WriterBJackson@aol.com or visit her Web site at www.brendajackson.net.

To all my readers who have fallen in love with the Westmoreland family. This one is for you.

Happy is the man that findeth wisdom, and the man that getteth understanding.

—*Proverbs* 3:13

One

$\mathbf{T}$he woman had a death grip on his thigh. The pain was almost unbearable but her hands touching him felt so damn good.

No longer satisfied with looking at her out of the corner of his eye, Stone Westmoreland slowly glanced over to stare at the woman, studying every single element about her. She was strapped in her seat as if the plane would crash unless she grabbed hold of something. Her eyes were shut tight and her breathing was irregular and it reminded him of the breathing pattern of a woman who'd just experienced the most satisfying orgasm. Just thinking about her touch aroused him....

He leaned back in his seat as the plane leveled off in the sky and closed his own eyes. With back-to-back book deadlines, it had been a long time since he'd been with a woman and a mere touch from her had sent his libido into overdrive.

He opened his eyes and took a shaky breath, hoping the month he would spend at his cousin's ranch in Montana, getting his thoughts together for a new book, would do him some good. At thirty-three, he and Durango were only a few months apart in age and had always been close. Then there was his uncle Corey who lived not far from Durango on a ranch high up in the mountains. Corey Westmoreland was his father's youngest brother who, at fifty-four, had retired as a park ranger after over thirty years of service.

Stone had fond memories of the summers he and his one sister, four brothers and six male cousins had shared visiting Uncle Corey. They had gained a great appreciation for the outdoors, as well as for wildlife. Their uncle always took his job as a park ranger seriously and his love for the wilderness had been contagious.

The one thing that stood out in Stone's mind about his uncle was that he never planned to marry. In fact, other than the women in the family, no other woman's foot had ever touched the soil of Corey's mountain. His uncle always said it was because he was so ornery and set in his ways that marriage wasn't for him. He much preferred living the life of a bachelor.

Stone's thoughts shifted to his brothers. This time last year all of them had been happy-go-lucky, enjoying every single minute of playing the field. Then the next thing you know, Dare, the eldest, got married and less than six months later, last month to be exact, his brother Thorn was marching down the aisle. Everyone in the family began ribbing Stone, saying since he was the third Westmoreland brother he would probably be next.

And he had been quick to tell them that hell would freeze over first.

He enjoyed being a bachelor too much to fall for any type of marriage trap. And although he would be the first to admit that the women his brothers had married were the best and more than worthy of their undying love and affection, he had decided a long time ago, just like Uncle Corey, that marriage wasn't for him. Not that he considered himself ornery or set in his ways; he just did not want to be responsible for anyone other than himself. He enjoyed the freedom to come and go whenever he pleased, and being a national, award-winning, bestselling author of action-thriller novels afforded him that luxury. He traveled all over the world to do research, and whenever he did date it was on his time and no one else's. For him women were a necessity, but only at certain times, and usually it wasn't difficult to find one who agreed to an affair on his terms.

To be completely honest, Stone had no issues with the concept of marriage, he just wasn't ready to take the plunge himself. He'd made a decision long ago to remain single after watching a good friend, who was also a bestselling author, become hopelessly in love and besotted with a woman. After getting married, Mark had decided that writing was not a priority in his life anymore. His focus had switched. He much preferred spending time with his wife instead of sitting at a computer all day. It was as if Mark had become Samson who'd gotten a hair cut. Once married, he had been zapped of his identity.

The thought that he could lose his desire to write over something called love totally unnerved Stone. Since publishing his first book at twenty-three, writing had become his life and he didn't intend for that to change. Doing so would mean losing control and the idea of losing that type of control on his life was something he couldn't handle.

Stone decided to check out the woman sitting beside him once more. Even with her eyes closed, he immediately liked what he saw. Shoulder-length dark brown hair and skin the color of dark coffee. She had a nice set of full lips and her nose was just the right fit for her face. She had long lashes and her cheeks were high. If she was wearing makeup, it was not very much. She was a natural beauty.

He glanced down at her hand, the one gripping his thigh. She was not wearing an engagement or wedding ring, which was good; and she had boarded the plane in Atlanta, which meant she either lived in the area or had come through the city to catch this connecting flight. Since they were on the same plane, unless she had another connecting flight, she was also bound for Montana.

His body tensed when he felt her grip tighten on his thigh. He inhaled deeply. If her hand moved even less than an inch, she would be clutching the most intimate part of him and he doubted she wanted to do that. Chances were she assumed her hand was gripping the armrest, so he decided he'd better let her know what was going on before he embarrassed them both.

He noticed that the sun, shining through the airplane window, hit her features at such an angle that they glowed. Even her hair appeared thick and luxurious and fanned her face in a way that made her look even more attractive.

Leaning over quietly, so as not to startle her, he breathed in her scent before getting a single word out of his mouth. It was a fragrance that turned him on even more than he already was. The aroma seemed entrenched into her skin and he was tempted to take his tongue and lick a portion of her bare neck to see if perhaps he could sample a taste of it.

Stone shook his head. Since when had he developed a fetish for a woman's skin? He enjoyed the art of kissing, like most men, but wanting to taste, nibble and devour a woman all over had never been something that interested him.

Until now.

He pushed the thought to the back of his mind, deciding it was too dangerous to even go there; he leaned closer and whispered softly in her ear, "The plane has leveled off so you can let go of me now."

She snapped open her eyes and quickly turned her head to meet his gaze. A part of him suddenly wished she hadn't done that. He found himself staring into the most beautiful set of brown eyes he had ever seen. They were perfect for the rest of her features and something in their dark depths made his body almost jerk in the seat.

She was simply gorgeous, although in truth there wasn't anything simple about it. She literally took his breath away. And, speaking of breath, he watched as she drew in a long, shaky one before glancing down at her left hand. She immediately snatched it off his thigh.

Awareness flashed in her eyes and total embarrassment appeared on her face. "Oh, oh, I'm so sorry. I didn't mean to touch you. I thought my hand was on the armrest. I—I didn't mean to act so improperly."

When Stone saw the degree of distress on her face he decided to assure her that he would survive. The last thing he wanted was for her to come unglued and get all flustered on him. And he really liked her accent. It was totally different from his Southern drawl and had the unmistakable inflection of a northeasterner. She was definitely someone from one of those New England States.

"Hey, no harm's done," he tried to say casually. "My name is Stone Westmoreland," he said, introducing himself and presenting his hand to her.

She still looked embarrassed when she took it and said, "And I'm Madison Winters."

He smiled. "Nice meeting you, Madison. Is this your first flight?"

She shook her head when he released her hand. "Nice meeting you, too, and no, this isn't my first flight, but I have a definite fear of flying. I try using other means of transportation whenever I can, but in this particular situation time is of the essence."

He nodded. "And where are you from?" he couldn't help but ask, her accent affecting him just as much as her touch had. Just listening to how she pronounced her words was a total turn-on.

"I'm from Boston. I was born and raised there."

He nodded again. "I'm from the Atlanta area," he decided to say when moments passed and she hadn't taken the liberty to ask. Whether it was from shyness or disinterest, he wasn't sure. But as far as he was concerned it didn't matter if she wasn't interested in him. He was definitely interested in her.

"I love visiting Atlanta," she said moments later. "I took my class on a field trip there once."

He raised a brow. "Your class?"

She smiled and his stomach flipped. "Yes, I'm a teacher. I teach music to sixth graders."

Stone smiled, surprised. He would never have figured her to be the artsy type. He remembered taking band when he was about eleven and learning to play the clarinet. His band teacher had looked nothing like her. "Must be interesting."

Her smile widened. "It is and I enjoy what I do."

He chuckled. "Yes, in this day and time it's good when a person can enjoy their work."

She stared at him for a second then asked, "And what type of work do you do?"

He hesitated before answering. As a bestselling author he used a pseudonym to ensure his privacy, but for some reason he felt comfortable being truthful with her. "I'm a fiction writer."

A smile tilted her lips. "Oh, how wonderful. Sorry, but I don't recall ever reading any of your books. What exactly do you write about?"

Stone chuckled. "I write action-thriller novels under the pseudonym of Rock Mason."

She blinked and then gasped. "You're Rock Mason? *The* Rock Mason?"

He smiled, glad that she had at least heard of Rock Mason. "Yes."

"Oh, my gosh! My mother has read every single book you've written. She is an avid fan of yours."

His smile widened. "What about you? Have you read any of my books?"

She gazed at him with regret. "No, I usually don't have time to read for pleasure, but from what I understand you're a gifted author."

"Thanks."

"A few of my girlfriends are in book clubs and they select your books to read and discuss whenever they hit the bookstores. You have quite a following in Boston. Have you ever visited there?"

"Yes, I did a book signing in Boston a couple of years ago and thought it was a beautiful city."

Madison beamed. "It is. I love Boston and can't imagine myself living anywhere else. I even attended Boston University because I didn't want to leave home."

At that moment they were interrupted as the flight attendant stopped to serve them drinks and a snack.

"So are you headed for Montana on business?" Stone asked. He remembered her saying something earlier about needing to get there rather quickly. He watched as she took a bite of her muffin and immediately felt his libido register the single crumb that clung to the side of her mouth. If that wasn't bad enough, she took a long sip of coffee and closed her eyes. Seconds later, as if the coffee was the best she'd ever tasted, she reopened her eyes. He saw the play of emotions across her face as she thought about his question.

"No, my visit to Montana is strictly personal." Then she studied him for a moment as if making a decision about something and said, "I'm going to Montana to find my mother."

Stone lifted a brow. "Oh? Is she missing?"

Madison leaned back against her seat, seemingly frustrated. "Yes. She and a couple of other women from Boston flew to Montana two weeks ago to tour Yellowstone National Park." She looked down and studied her coffee before adding in a low voice, "All the other women returned except my mother."

He heard the deep concern in her voice. "Have you heard from her?"

She nodded her head. "Yes. She left a message on my answering machine letting me know that she had decided to extend her vacation another two weeks."

A part of Madison wondered why she was disclosing such information to Stone, a virtual stranger. The only reason she could come up with was that she needed to talk to someone and Stone Westmoreland seemed like a nice enough guy to listen. Besides, she needed an unbiased ear.

"She left a message that she's extending her vacation yet you're going to Montana to look for her anyway?"

Stone's question, and the way he had asked it, let her know he didn't understand. "Yes, because there's a man involved."

He nodded slowly. "Oh, I see."

Frankly, he really didn't see at all and evidently his expression revealed as much because she then said, "You might not think there's reason for concern, Mr. Westmoreland, but—"

"Stone. Please call me Stone."

She smiled. "All right." Then she started explaining herself again. "There is good reason for my concern, Stone. My mother hasn't done anything like this before."

He nodded again. "So you think that perhaps there has been some sort of foul play?"

She shook her head, denying that possibility. "No, I think it has something to do with her going through some sort of midlife crisis. She turned fifty a couple of months ago, and until that time she was completely normal."

Stone took a sip of his coffee. He remembered what happened when his mother turned fifty. She decided that she wanted to go back to school and start working outside of the home. His father almost had a fit because he was one of those traditional men who believed a woman's work was in the home raising kids. But his mother had made up her mind about what she wanted to do and nothing was going to stop her. Since his baby sister, Delaney, had gone off to college and there weren't any kids left at home to raise, his father had finally given in.

He shifted his thoughts to Madison's mother. Personally, he saw nothing abnormal with a woman disappearing in the wilds of Montana with a man, if that's what she wanted to do. However, from the worried expression on Madison's face, she evidently thought otherwise.

"So what do you plan on doing when you find her?" he asked curiously. After all, she was still the daughter and her mother was still the mother. He had learned from experience that parents felt they could do whatever pleased them without any interference from their children. At least that had always been the case with his mother and father, and he thought they were the greatest parents in the world.

"I'm going to try and talk some sense into her, of course," Madison said, her lips tightening in determination. "My father died of a heart attack over ten years ago, and my mother has been a widow since that time. She is the most staid, levelheaded and sensible person you could ever meet."

She sighed deeply then added, "Taking off with a man she doesn't know, whom she only met one night at dinner, doesn't make sense and it's so unlike her."

Stone's action-thriller mind went to work. "And you're positive she went off with this man willingly?"

He watched a clearly frustrated Madison take another sip of her coffee before answering. "Yes, there were witnesses, including the ladies who accompanied her on the trip. They said she simply packed one morning and announced that the guy was coming for her and she would be spending the rest of the time with him and to let me know she had decided to extend her trip. Of course I couldn't believe it and had all but called in the FBI before I got her phone call. Unfortunately, I wasn't at home when she called so we didn't talk, but her message clearly said that she was all right and was extending her vacation another two weeks and not to worry about her. But of course I'm worried."

Stone thought that was pretty evident. "Can she take additional time off from her job like that?" he asked, curious with everything Madison was telling him.

"Yes. My mother retired as a hospital administrator last year and owns a day-care center for the elderly. She has an excellent staff. Over the past couple of months she's been spending less time at the office and doing a lot of charity work in the community. She's really big into that."

Stone leaned back in his seat. "Do you have an idea where you plan to look? Montana is a huge place."

"I've made reservations at this dude ranch outside of Bozeman called the Silver Arrow. Have you ever heard of it?"

Stone smiled. Yes, he had. In fact, the Silver Arrow Dude Ranch was only a short distance from Durango's place. He was rather pleased that he and Madison would be in close proximity to each other. "I know exactly where it is. In fact, it's not far from where I'll be staying. The two of us will practically be neighbors."

She smiled like the thought of that pleased her. Or maybe it was wishful thinking on his part, Stone thought as his gaze centered on her lips.

"I've made plans for a tour guide to take me up into the mountains after I'm settled," she said, breaking into his thoughts.

Stone lifted a brow. "Up into the mountains?"

"Yes, that's where the man has taken my mother."

He paused in the act of taking a bite of his muffin. "This man took your mother up into the mountains?" At her nod he then asked, "Why?"

"Because that's where he lives."

After chewing a morsel of the muffin, Stone inquired, "The guy actually lives in the mountains?" He took a swallow of coffee, thinking he'd always thought his uncle Corey was the only man brave enough to forgo civilization and live high up in the mountains. While he worked as a park ranger, Corey Westmoreland stayed in the lowlands, making the trip into the mountains on his days off.

"Yes, according to the information I was able to find, he lives on this huge mountain," Madison said, interrupting his thoughts. "The man is a retired park ranger. I don't have his full name but I understand he's well known in those parts and goes by Carl, Cole, Cord or something like that."

A portion of Stone's coffee went down the wrong pipe and he began coughing to clear his throat.

"Stone, are you all right?" Madison asked in concern.

Stone looked at her, not sure if he was all right or not. The man she had just described sounded a lot like his uncle Corey.

But a woman on Corey's mountain?

He cleared this throat thoroughly before asking his next question. He met her gaze, hoping he had not heard her correctly. "Are you saying that some guy who is a retired park ranger and who owns a ranch high up in the mountains is the person your mother ran off with?"

After wiping her mouth with a napkin, Madison nodded her head. "Yes. Can you imagine anything so ridiculous?"

No. In all honesty I can't, if we're talking about the same person. Stone thought about what she had told him. He then considered everything he knew about his uncle, especially how he felt about a woman ever setting foot on his beloved mountain.

He then answered Madison as honestly as he knew how. "No, I can't imagine anything so ridiculous."

She must have talked the man to death, Madison thought, glancing over at Stone a short while later. Conversation between them had dwindled off and he was leaning back in his seat, his head tipped back against the headrest, his eyes closed either in sleep or deep thought.

She couldn't help but take this opportunity to examine him.

If a man could be described as beautiful, it would be him. He was more handsome than any man had a right to be. She could easily tell that he had broad shoulders and although he was sitting down there was no doubt in her mind that he probably had pretty lean hips. But what captivated her most about him were his dark almond-shaped eyes and she wished they weren't closed so she could gaze into them some more.

They were as dark as midnight and, when he had looked at her, it was as if he could see everything, right deep into her very soul. Then there was his neatly trimmed curly black hair that was cut low, his high cheekbones and his beautifully full lips that had almost melted her in her seat when he had smiled. And the healthy texture of his chestnut skin tempted her to touch it to see if it was really soft as cotton.

For the first time, her mind was not focused on the fact that she was on a plane, but on the fact that she was sitting next to the most gorgeous man she had ever seen. Ordinarily, she would be the last person to notice a man after what Cedric had done to her a couple of years ago. Finding out the man you were about to marry was having an affair was painful to say the least. Since then she had decided that no man was worth the trouble. Some people were just meant to be alone.

She settled back in her seat, frowning as she wondered if the reason her mother had taken off with a man was because she had been tired of living alone. Abby Winters had been widowed for over ten years, and Madison knew her father's death had not been easy on her. She'd also known, even though her mother had refused to discuss it, that her parents had not had a happy marriage. All it had taken was a weekend spent in the home of a high school friend, whose parents were still very much in love, to notice things she didn't see at home. Her father had never kissed her mother before leaving for work, nor had they exchanged funny looking smiles across the dinner table when they thought no one was watching.

Her parents had been highly educated people: Harvard graduates. Somehow over the years they had become absorbed in their individual careers. Although there was no doubt in her mind that they had loved her, it was clearly obvious that at some point they had stopped loving each other.

It seemed they had pretty much accepted a loveless marriage. Even after her father's death, her mother still didn't date, although Madison knew several men had asked her out once or twice.

That's what made Abby Winters' actions now so baffling and unacceptable. What was it about the man that had captured her mother's interest enough to do something as outrageous as going off with him to his mountain? As she had told Stone, her mother was the most rational person she knew, so it had to be some sort of midlife crisis. There was no other explanation for it.

And what would she say to her mother when she saw her? That was a question for which she had no answer. The only thing she knew for certain was that she was determined to talk some sense into her. Fifty-year-old women just did not run off with men they didn't know.

Madison shook her head. She was twenty-five and she would never take up with some man she didn't know, even someone as good looking as Stone. She quickly glanced over at him and had to admit that taking off with him was definitely a tempting thought.

A *very* tempting thought.

She pushed the thought aside, thinking that one Winters woman acting impulsive and irrational was enough.

What if the man Madison Winters had described was really Uncle Corey?

With his eyes closed, that question continued to plague Stone's mind. At the moment he was pretending to be asleep, not wanting Madison to see his inner turmoil. Since the plane was at an altitude where he could use a mobile phone, he considered calling Durango to find out if Corey had abducted the woman. Durango, who was also a park ranger, had moved to Montana to attend college and joined the profession that their uncle had loved so much.

Durango had lived with Corey until he had saved up enough to purchase his own land. But calling Durango was not an option, not with Madison sitting next to him. Although she would try not to eavesdrop, there was no way she would not overhear his every word. He had no choice but to wait until the plane landed to question Durango. He hoped like hell that he was wrong and there was another retired park ranger who lived high in the mountains and whose name began with the letter C.

Stone breathed in slowly. Madison's scent was getting to him again. If he were completely honest he would admit that his blood had begun stirring the moment she had sat next to him on the flight. He had tried ignoring her by concentrating on the activities outside the plane window as the airline crew prepared for takeoff, and had pretty much dismissed her from his mind until she had touched him.

Aroused him was a much better word.

He sighed deeply. This would definitely be one flight he would not forget in a long time. He couldn't help but open his eyes and glance over at her. Her eyes were closed, her lips were parted and she was breathing at an even pace. Unlike before, she was now resting peacefully and had somehow taken her mind off her fear of flying, and a part of him felt good about that. He didn't want to dwell on the protective instincts he was developing for her. Perhaps he felt this way because she reminded him of his baby sister, Delaney.

A lazy smile touched his lips. As the only girl constantly surrounded by five older brothers and six older male cousins, Delaney had been overprotected most of her life. But after graduating from medical school she had pulled a fast one on everyone and had sneaked away to a secluded cabin in the North Carolina mountains for rest and relaxation, only to discover the mountain retreat was already occupied. A visiting desert sheikh, who'd had the same idea about rest and relaxation, had been ensconced in the cabin when she'd arrived. During the course of their "vacation," the two fell in love and now his baby sister was a princess living in the Middle East.

Delaney was presently in the States with her family to finish her residency at a hospital in Kentucky. He enjoyed seeing his one-year-old nephew Ari and had to admit that his sister's husband, Sheikh Jamal Ari Yasir, had grown on him and his brothers, and now he was as welcome a sight as Delaney. Stone knew Jamal loved his sister immensely.

He looked around the plane, wishing there was some way he could walk around and stretch his stiff muscles, but knew that would mean waking Madison to reach the aisle, and he didn't want to do that for fear she would start talking again about the man who could be his uncle. Until he got some answers from Durango, the last thing he wanted to do was come across as if he were deceiving her.

He glanced over at her once more and admired her beauty. To his way of thinking, Madison Winters was a woman no man in his right mind would want to deceive.

Two

The landing was smooth and as the plane taxied up to the terminal, Madison breathed a sigh of relief to be back on the ground. She unbuckled her seat belt and watched as the other passengers wasted little time getting out of their seats and gathering their belongings from the overhead compartments. Some people were moving quickly to catch connecting flights, while others appeared eager to be reunited with the loved ones waiting for them.

"Do you need help getting anything?"

She turned and met Stone's gaze. His voice was low, deep and seductive, and reminded her of the husky baritone of the singer Barry White. The rhythm of her heart increased.

"No, I can manage, but thanks for asking. If you don't

mind, I'll wait until the plane empties before getting off. If you need to get by I can move out of your way."

"No, I'm in no hurry, either. I doubt my cousin is here to pick me up since he's never on time." He smiled. "But then he just might surprise me this time."

His smile did funny things to her insides, Madison thought, glancing around to see how many people were left to get off the plane. The best thing to do would be to get as far away from Stone Westmoreland as soon as she could. The man messed with her ability to think straight and, for the moment, finding her mother needed her full concentration.

"Do you have transportation to the Silver Arrow ranch?"

Again she met his gaze. "Yes. I was told they would be sending someone for me."

Stone nodded. "Too bad. I was going to offer you a ride. I'm sure Durango wouldn't mind dropping you off since it's on the way."

Madison lifted a brow. "Durango?"

Stone smiled. "Yes, my cousin Durango. He's a park ranger at Yellowstone National Park."

Stone watched her eyes grow wide. "A park ranger? Then there's a chance he might know the man my mother took off with," she said excitedly.

Durango might know him better than you think, Stone wanted to say but didn't. Although the man she had described sounded a lot like Corey, it was still hard for Stone to believe that his uncle had actually taken a woman to his mountain. Stone never knew the full story why Corey had written off any kind of permanent relationship with a woman, he only knew that he had. "Yes, there is that possibility," Stone finally said.

"Then, if you don't mind, I'd like to ask him about it."

"No, I don't mind." Stone only hoped that he would get the chance to speak to Durango first.

"The way is clear to go now."

Madison's words recaptured his attention. He watched as she stood and eased out into the aisle. Opening the overhead compartment, she pulled out an overnight bag, a brand he recognized immediately as being Louis Vuitton. He smiled, remembering that he had given his sister Delaney a Louis Vuitton purse as a graduation present when she had earned her medical degree. He had been amazed at how much the item had cost, but when he had seen how happy the gift had made Delaney, the amount he'd spent had been well worth it.

Delaney had once explained that you could tell just how polished and classy a woman was by the purse she carried. If that was the case, Madison Winters was one hell of a polished and classy woman because she was sporting a Louis Vuitton purse, as well. He stood up and followed her into the aisle.

Madison looked ahead and thought the aisle of the plane seemed a hundred miles long. When they had to stop abruptly for the line of people moving slowly ahead of them, Stone automatically placed his hands at her waist to keep her from losing her balance.

She turned and gazed over her shoulder at him. "Thanks, Stone."

"My pleasure."

She smiled thinking it wasn't his pleasure alone. She felt his hard, solid chest pressed against her back and, when he placed his hands on her waist, she was acutely aware of the strength in his touch. He was a tall man. She wasn't conscious of just how tall until he stood up. He towered over her and when she tilted her head back to thank him, he met her gaze. The look in his eyes nearly took her breath away.

Although he wasn't wearing a wedding ring, there was no way a man who looked this good could be unattached, she thought. A probing query entered her mind. He'd said his cousin Durango would be picking him up. Would there be a special lady waiting for him, as well? In her opinion, Stone Westmoreland had a magnetic, compelling charm that made him an irresistible force to reckon with.

When they left the plane, the two of them walked side by side through the ramp corridor toward the arrival area. "So, how long do you plan to stay in Montana?" Stone asked.

Madison could tell he had shortened his stride to stay level with her. She glanced over at him, met his gaze and tried to ignore the way her breasts tingled against the fabric of her blouse. "I'll stay until I find my mother and talk to her. I'm hoping it won't take long. According to Mr. Jamison, who owns the Silver Arrow, the cabin where my mother is staying is not far, but since it's located in the mountains getting there will be difficult. He's arranging for someone to take me by car as far as possible, then the rest will be done on horseback."

Stone lifted a brow and scrutinized her with an odd stare. "You ride?"

Madison's lips curved into a smile. "Yes. Growing up I

took riding lessons. I'm sure climbing up a mountain will be far more challenging than just prancing a mare around a riding track, but I think I'll be able to manage."

Stone wasn't so sure. She seemed too refined and delicate to sit on a horse for a trip into the rugged mountains.

"That's something I don't understand."

Her words interrupted his thoughts. "What?"

"How my mother got up the mountain. I don't think she's ever ridden a horse. My dad tried getting her to take riding lessons when I took mine but she refused."

Stone nodded. "They probably rode double. Although it might be strenuous, it's possible on a good, strong horse," he said. He could just imagine Madison sitting behind him on horseback. He took a deep, calming breath as he thought about her arms wrapped around him when she hung on to him, and the feel of her breasts pressed against his back while her scent filled his nostrils.

He winced. He had to stop thinking about her like this. He was in Montana to research a book, not to get involved in a serious affair or a nonserious one for that matter. However, he had to admit that the thought of it, especially with Madison as a partner, was a damn good one.

Together they walked to the area where they needed to claim their luggage. Stone scanned the crowd for Durango and wasn't surprised when he didn't see him. He assisted Madison in pulling her luggage off the conveyor belt before getting his bags.

"Thanks for making my flight enjoyable. Because of you I was able to take my mind off my fear of flying."

He decided not to say that, on the same note, thanks to her, he was reminded just how long it had been since he'd had a woman. "Do you see the person who's supposed to be picking you up?" he asked glancing around.

"No. Maybe I should call. Will you excuse me while I use that courtesy phone over there?"

"Sure."

Stone watched her walk to the phone. In a tailored pantsuit that fit her body to perfection, she looked totally out of place in Bozeman, Montana. All the other women were wearing jeans and shirts, and she was dressed like she was attending a high priority business meeting somewhere. He appreciated the sway of her hips when she walked and how her hair brushed against her shoulders with every step she took.

"You can't be left alone one minute before you're checking out a woman, Stone. Even one who has 'city girl' written all over her."

Stone switched his attention from Madison to the man who had suddenly appeared by his side: his cousin Durango. "I sat by her on the plane from Atlanta. She's nice."

Durango chuckled as a wide grin covered his face. "All women are nice."

Stone shook his head. Everyone in the family knew that, like his brother Storm, Durango was a ladies' man, a player of the first degree and, like Stone and their uncle Corey, Durango had no intention of ever settling down. And speaking of Corey....

"When was the last time you saw Uncle Corey?" Stone decided to cut to the chase and ask. He knew that Durango kept up with their uncle's comings and goings. If there was some woman on Corey's mountain, Durango would know about it.

The grin suddenly disappeared from Durango's face;

not a good sign as far as Stone was concerned. "Funny you should ask," Durango said frowning. "I haven't seen him for a week and I know for a fact he has a woman up there on his mountain."

That wasn't what Stone wanted to hear. "Are you sure?"

"Yes, I'm sure. I saw her myself when they were passing through. She's a nice-looking woman, probably in her late forties and talks with one of those northern accents. They've been up on that mountain for almost a week now and Corey won't answer the phone or return my calls. It makes me wonder what's going on up there and how this woman got such special privileges. I couldn't believe he broke his long-standing rule about a woman on his mountain."

Stone leaned back against the railing. His mind was reeling and he needed to make sure he had heard everything Durango was telling him correctly. "You're saying that Corey actually has a woman on his mountain?"

"Yes, and she's not a long-lost relative, either, because I asked. Besides, it was obvious she wasn't related by the way they were acting. He couldn't wait to leave my place to head into the mountains and it doesn't appear he's bringing her down anytime soon."

Stone rubbed a hand down his face. "And you're sure you don't know who she is?"

Durango's frown deepened. "No, I don't know who she is, Stone, other than the fact he was calling her Abby. But you better believe that this Abby woman has hooked him in good, and I mean real good."

When the crowd standing directly behind Durango shifted, Stone noticed that Madison had finished her call and had walked up. From the expression on her face it was obvious that she had pretty much overheard most of what Durango had said.

Aw hell!

Durango noticed that Stone's gaze was fixed on something behind him and turned around. He smiled when he looked into the face of the woman Stone had been checking out earlier. He grinned. No wonder his cousin was taken with the woman, she was definitely a looker. Too bad Stone had met her first, because she was definitely someone who would have interested him.

He started to speak and introduce himself, since it seemed Stone had suddenly lost his voice. But something made him pause. Durango had dealt with enough women to know when they weren't happy about something and it was obvious this woman was angry, royally pissed off. And her words stopped him dead in his tracks.

"I believe the woman the two of you are discussing is my mother."

It wasn't hard to tell the two men were related, Madison thought, glancing up at them. Both were tall, extremely handsome and well built. Then there were the similarities in their facial features that also proved a family connection. They possessed the same close-cropped curly black hair, chestnut coloring, dark intense eyes and generous, well-defined mouths.

And both of them could wear a pair of jeans and a chambray shirt like nobody's business.

Madison inwardly admitted that, had she met the other man before Stone, she probably would have felt the same attraction to him, the same pull. However, she thought there was a gentleness and tenderness in Stone's eyes that she didn't easily see in the other man's.

She could tell her statement took the other man by surprise but when she glanced over at Stone, it was obvious that what she'd said hadn't surprised him, which meant he had known or at least suspected the identity of her mother's abductor all along.

She lifted a brow and leveled a pointed gaze at Stone. She had trusted him enough to discuss her mother with him openly, because she had needed someone to talk to, and talking to him had calmed her fears of flying and had also helped her to think through her mother's situation. If Stone had suspected the people she had been talking about were his uncle and her mother, why hadn't he said something?

Stone read the questions in Madison's eyes. "I didn't know, Madison, or at least I wasn't a hundred percent certain," he said in a low and calm voice. "And although I thought there was a possibility the man was my uncle Corey, I didn't want to upset you any more than you already were by adding my speculations."

Madison released a deep sigh. His reason for not telling her did make sense. "All right," she said softly. "So, what do we do now?"

Durango lifted a confused brow and looked at Stone and then back at Madison. "Why should we do anything? When they're ready they'll come back down the mountain."

Stone stifled a grin at the angry look Madison gave Durango. His cousin, the player, didn't have a snowball's chance in hell of winning this particular woman over. He doubted Madison got upset about anything or with anyone too often, but he could tell Durango was making her break her record. Durango had a rather rough way of dealing with women. He wasn't used to the soft and gentle approach. Yet the way women were still drawn to him defied logic.

"This is my cousin, Durango Westmoreland, Madison," Stone decided to say when silence, annoyance and irritation settled between Durango and Madison.

"And when Durango gives himself time to think logically, I'm sure he'll understand your concern for your mother's well-being. And although Durango and I both know that our uncle Corey would never do anything to harm your mother, we can certainly understand your desire to see for yourself that she's fine."

Stone watched a slow smile touched Durango's lips. From childhood they had always been able to read between the lines of each other's words. Stone was letting Durango know, in a subtle way, that he wanted him on his best behavior and to clean up his act.

"I apologize if what I said upset you, Madison," Durango said, offering her his hand in a firm handshake. "I wasn't aware that you thought your mother was in harm's way. If that's the case, we'll certainly do whatever needs to be done to arrest your fears. And let me be the first to welcome you to Montana."

Stone rolled his eyes. No one, he thought, could go from being a pain in the ass to irresistibly charming in a blink of an eye like Durango. Stone watched the warmth return to Madison's eyes and she smiled. Although that smile wasn't directed at him, a riot of emotions clamored through him nonetheless.

"Now that we have all that settled," he decided to speak

up and say, "how about the three of us going somewhere to talk? Durango, you mentioned that you had met Madison's mother when Uncle Corey made a stop at your place."

A smile was plastered on Durango's face when he said, "Yes, and I even talked to her for a few minutes while Corey was loading up on supplies. I could tell she was a real classy, well-bred lady."

Madison nodded. She appreciated his comments although her mother's actions were showing another side of her. "Stone is right. I'd like to get to the Silver Arrow and unpack and freshen up, but as soon as I can, I'd like to meet with you and ask you a few more questions."

Durango quickly glanced over at Stone and Stone deciphered the message in his eyes. There were some things Madison was probably better off not knowing about her mother and their uncle.

Stone nodded and Durango caught his drift and returned his attention to Madison and said, "Sure, that will be fine, Madison. Is someone coming to pick you up from the Silver Arrow or can I give you a lift?"

"I don't want to put you to any trouble, Mr. Westmoreland."

Durango grinned again. "Just call me Durango and there's no trouble. The Silver Arrow is on the way to my ranch and is nicely situated between Bozeman and Yellowstone, and only a stone's throw away from the Wyoming line."

Madison nodded. "Thanks, I'll be glad to take you up on your offer. The man who answered the phone at the Silver Arrow said the guy who usually picks up his guests was ill and he was trying to find a replacement."

Durango reached out to take the luggage out of her hand. "Then consider it done."

Madison sat in the vehicle's back seat. Although she hated being in Montana, she couldn't overlook the beauty of this beautiful June day, as well as the vast country surrounding her. It was magnificent and left her utterly speechless. The Rocky Mountains were all around and the meadows were drenched with wildflowers: Red Indian Paintbrush and an assortment of other flowering plants. She had always heard about the beauty of being under a Montana sky and now she was experiencing it firsthand.

They were traveling down a two-lane stretch of highway; she knew they were a stone's throw away from Yellowstone National Park and hoped that she could tour the park before returning to Boston.

At the airport, after Stone and Durango had helped with her luggage, they had walked out to where Durango's SUV was parked in a "no parking zone" with its caution lights flashing. She smiled when she saw he was driving a nice, sleek, shiny black Dodge Durango.

Stone leaned over and whispered in her ear that Durango owned a Dodge Durango because he was conceited enough to think Dodge had named the vehicle after him. Durango, she knew, had heard Stone's comment and had merely laughed it off, and she could immediately feel the closeness between the two men.

"So how long do you think you're going to stay in Montana after meeting with your mother, Madison?" Stone asked, glancing at her over his shoulder. It was easy to see how captivated she was with the beauty of the land surrounding them. Earlier, she had said that she would probably only be in Montana long enough to talk to her mother, but he knew that Montana had a way of growing on you. And he had to admit that there was something about Madison that was growing on him. It was obvious that she had some real concerns about her mother and more than anything he wanted to help her resolve them.

He watched as she switched her gaze from the scenery to him. "I know what I said earlier, but now I'm not sure. I had planned to leave as soon as I had talked to my mother but I might decide to hang around awhile. This place is beautiful," she said, taking a quick glance out of the window again.

She turned back to him to add, "Since school is out for the summer I can enjoy myself. I seldom take vacations during the summer months. Usually I give private music lessons, so this is a really nice break, although I wished it was a planned trip rather than an unplanned one."

Stone really didn't care about the reason she was in Montana, he was just glad that she was. He hoped things worked out between her and her mother but it seemed that Madison had never heard of anyone acting out of character. He had a feeling that, in the world she was used to, things went according to plan and as expected.

He smiled inwardly. In that case, his family would take some getting used to if she ever met them. His father had two brothers. Of the three siblings, their uncle Corey was the only single one. Never having been married and the youngest of the three, he had been a surrogate father to his eleven nephews and one niece.

Corey had left Atlanta to attend Montana State University and fell in love with the land. Once he had a job as a park ranger with Yellowstone National Park, he made the state his permanent home. By the time he retired a year ago, he had been president of the Association of National Park Rangers for the past five years and had accumulated a vast amount of land.

"Well, if you decide to stick around I'd like to show you the sights. I spent a lot of time here as a kid while visiting my uncle Corey and know my way around pretty well."

A smile touched the corners of Madison's mouth. "Thanks. I might take you up on that." She then asked quietly, "Just what type of person is your uncle Corey? I know Durango said he was harmless and trustworthy, but I'm trying to come to grips with what there is about him that made my mother act so unlike herself."

Stone glanced over at Durango and saw the smile that tilted his cousin's lips; he was grateful that Durango, for once, had the decency to keep quiet. The rumor that Uncle Corey could make even the First Lady stop being a lady was something Madison didn't need to know. Chances were, if she asked anyone working at the Silver Arrow about Corey they would gladly enlighten her since his reputation was legendary.

Stone didn't really know what he could tell her; her mother being on his uncle's mountain didn't make much sense to him, either. He couldn't wait to get Durango alone to get the full story.

"I guess there are times when things happen that defy logic, Madison, and it appears this is the case with your mother and Uncle Corey. Just like your mother's actions are unusual, his actions are unusual, too. For as long as I've known him, which has been for all of my thirty-three years, he's been pretty much of a loner; preferring not to marry and spending most of his time when he wasn't at Yellowstone up on his mountain. And he's always had a rule about taking women up there."

Madison lifted a brow. "And what rule is that?"

Stone smiled. "That it would never happen. Other than female family members, there has never been a woman on his mountain. There must have been something about your mother to make him change his way of thinking about that."

A thought crossed Stone's mind. "Is there a chance that my uncle and your mother knew each other before?"

Madison frowned. That thought had crossed her mind but she didn't see how that could be. "I guess anything is possible. That would certainly explain things somewhat if it were true. But I don't see how that could be possible unless your uncle had visited Boston. My parents dated all through high school and college, and married right after graduation. I was born two years later." She decided not to mention the unhappy marriage her parents had shared even though they had tried to pretend otherwise.

"Then there could be another reason for their madness," Stone said softly, reclaiming her attention, casting a sideways glance.

She looked at him, squinting against the sun that shone through the vehicle window. "And what reason is that?"

"Instant attraction."

Stone watched as Madison immediately parted her lips to refute such a thing was possible, then she closed them tight. She had to know that such a thing was possible because the two of them had experienced that same attraction on the plane, so to deny such a thing existed would be dishonest.

Moments later she said, "I'm sure that's possible but can it be that powerful to make a levelheaded person become impulsive and irrational?"

Stone chuckled. "Trust me, Madison, I've seen it happen." One day he would prove his point by telling her about his two brothers who'd recently married. He didn't count his sister's marriage as anything unusual, since Delaney had always looked at things through rose-colored eyes, which was the main reason he and his brothers had been so overprotective of her during her dating years.

But his brothers Dare and Thorn had been dead set against marrying anytime soon, if ever. He clearly understood why Dare had wed since Shelly had been Dare's true love. When she had returned to town after having been gone ten years, and with a son Dare hadn't known existed, it had been understandable that the two would get back together and make a home for their child. But a sense of obligation had nothing to do with Dare's marriage to Shelly. His brother loved Shelly, plain and simple.

Now there hadn't been anything plain and simple about Thorn's marriage to Tara. Thorn was the last Westmoreland anyone expected to marry and he was a prime example of what instant attraction could do to you if you weren't careful.

"Well, I can't imagine anything like that happening with my mother," Madison said defiantly, recapturing Stone's attention. "Does your uncle have a phone up on his mountain?"

Stone nodded his head. "Yes."

"Then I need the number. I want to call my mother and let her know I'm on my way up there."

Durango, who had been quiet all this time, ended his silence with a chuckle. "You might have a problem reaching them," he said, not taking his eyes off the road.

"Why?" Madison asked curiously. "Are the phone lines down or something?"

"No, but I've tried calling Uncle Corey for the past several days to remind him that Stone was coming for a visit and he's not answering his phone."

Madison arched a dark brow. "He's not answering his phone? But—but what if something has happened to them and they can't get to the phone. What if—"

"They don't want to be disturbed, Madison?" Stone suggested. He saw her eyes shift from the back of Durango's head over to him. He could tell from her expression that his comment had conjured up numerous possibilities in her mind, but there was no hope for it. At some point she needed to accept that her mother had decided to extend her vacation by two weeks because she had wanted to, and not because she had been forced to. As far as Stone was concerned, the same held true with Madison's mother being on that mountain. It didn't seem that his uncle had forced the woman, so chances were she was just where she wanted to be. Sooner or later Madison would have to realize that.

She didn't answer his question. Instead she turned back to the car window and looked out at the scenery again. Stone inhaled deeply and turned back around in his seat. At least he had her thinking and for the moment perhaps that was the best thing.

Three

What if Mom doesn't want to be disturbed like Stone suggested?

That thought ran through Madison's mind as she studied the mountains and the ripened green pastures they passed. She couldn't help but think of all the things she knew about her mother.

The two of them were close and always had been, but there were some things a mother didn't share with a daughter and Madison was smart enough to know that. It came as no surprise that she had never thought of her mother as a sensual being. To her, she was simply Mom, although she had always thought her mother was a very beautiful woman.

Stone's comment was forcing her to see her mother through different eyes. One thing she knew for certain was that, since her father's death, her mother hadn't shown any interest in a man, and Madison had never given any thought as to whether that was a good thing or not. Usually, when Abby Winters went to social functions, she attended with Ron Carmichael, a widower who had been her father's business partner, or she would attend with some other family friend.

Although both Durango and Stone had been too polite to state the obvious, it seemed pretty clear that her mother and their uncle Corey were on his mountain engaging in some sort of an illicit affair. And if that was the case, Madison was determined to find out how Corey Westmoreland had tempted her mother to behave in such a manner.

She also knew that, although neither men had voiced it, they probably thought she had taken things a little too far in coming after her mother, and especially when she'd been told her mother was fine. But a part of her had to see for herself. She had to talk to her mother.

And she had to understand, or at least try to understand. What had possessed her mother to do what she did? She had to believe there had to be a good reason.

She licked her lips as they suddenly felt dry. When Stone had talked about instant attraction, she had known just what he'd meant. From the moment she had opened her eyes on the plane to gaze into the dark depths of his, she had been attracted to him in a way she had never experienced before. And she was still attracted to him. Every time he looked at her, she felt a funny feeling inside that started in her breastbone and quickly moved down her body to settle right smack in the center between her legs. She was drawn to Stone. It was Stone who had her breathing fast just thinking how she had touched him intimately on the plane without knowing it. She felt a sudden tingling in her hand when she thought about just where it had been. And the first time he had spoken to her, she had immediately become mesmerized by the sound of his voice.

She sighed deeply. Considering her current state, she needed to get to the Silver Arrow, check into her cabin and pull herself together as soon as possible. She had to remember that she was here for one reason and for one reason only. It had nothing to do with Stone and everything to do with her mother.

But…once the issue of her mother's state of mind was resolved, she couldn't help but think of all the very tempting possibilities.

"You and Durango didn't have to help with my luggage, Stone," Madison said as she watched him place the last piece next to her bed. Once they had arrived at the Silver Arrow, the two men had been adamant about helping her instead of letting the ranch hands do it.

The ranch consisted of numerous rustic cabins that were located some distance away from the main house for privacy. Guy Jamison, the owner, had said he would give her a tour of the ranch once she got settled. He also told her the time dinner would be served and said he was waiting to hear back from the man who'd agreed to be her tour guide up to the mountains.

The cabin she had been given was tucked beneath a cluster of trees and appeared more secluded than the others. Durango bid her goodbye and left after helping Stone with her bags. He went to wait outside in the SUV.

She glanced around, trying to get her mind off Stone and

how good he looked standing in the middle of the room. In an attempt not to notice him, she let her gaze float across the décor and furnishings of the cabin. There was a dark oak bureau, dressing table and two nightstands on either side of the biggest bed she had ever seen. It appeared larger than king size and the printed covers made it look very welcoming and comfortable. She also took note of the matching curtains at the windows and frontier-printed rugs on the floor.

"Would you like to join me and Durango for dinner later?"

Madison met Stone's gaze. The attraction that had been there from the beginning was overcharging the room, blazing the distance between them and making her heart pound faster in her chest. Should she have dinner with him? He had indicated they wouldn't be alone since Durango would be joining them. And what if Durango wasn't joining them? Should she hesitate in accepting his offer just because he turned her on? But then she had more questions for Durango about her mother and Corey Westmoreland, and he'd said she could come over to his place.

She took a deep breath, deciding to be upfront with Stone since she couldn't deny the obvious. "The only reason I'm here is because of my mother, Stone, and when I resolve that issue, I'll decide if I want anything out of this trip for myself. Chances are I won't and will return to Boston as soon as I can."

He nodded, understanding what she was saying. "All right," he said and slowly crossed the distance separating them. "If that speech was to let me know you need time to figure things out, that's fine. Take all the time you need."

He needed time to figure things out, as well. Why did

she turn him on like no other woman he knew and why at that very moment was the need to taste her about to make him lose his mind? In the past, his writing had always taken center stage in his life. He had lived more or less through his characters, knowing their fears, conflicts and deep-rooted and often chilling adventures. Transferring his thoughts from his mind to paper had been all consuming and the need to block off everything and anyone had been essential. His only goal had been to deliver, on every occasion, what readers expected from a Rock Mason book and he, without exception, had happily obliged them. The last thing he had to spare while working on a book was time for a woman, and in the past that was something he understood and accepted. But he knew he would be hard pressed to understand and accept anything about this situation with Madison Winters other than the fact that he wanted her. Pure and simple.

"Can I leave you with something to think about?" he asked quietly. The afternoon light that was flowing in through the only window in the cabin was casting a shadow on her features, but instead of dimming her allure, the light brought Madison's beauty even more into focus. He swallowed hard, steeling his resolve, only to discover that when it came to this woman he didn't have any.

Madison met Stone's gaze, holding it tightly. Intensely. She wondered what he was giving her time to think about. Did he have words of wisdom to share or was there something else? Her mind began whirling at all the possibilities and, heaven help her, but a part of her wished there was something else. She contemplated him for a long moment, wondering how she should respond if what he had in mind was the latter. Any physical contact, no matter how casual, wasn't a good idea since they had just met that day. Then she remembered that the first phase of physical contact had taken place the moment she had touched him on the plane, although the contact hadn't been intentional. But still, contact had been made and she hadn't been the same since.

And she could be honest enough with herself to admit that her mind had been made up about Stone the moment she had stepped off the plane with him. There was something about him that denoted a sense of honor, something rarely seen in a man these days.

He was the silent type with the word sexy oozing out of every pore on his body. She had never met a man like him before and doubted that she would again. For some reason she felt she could trust him, although blindly placing her trust in a man had been precisely how her heart had been broken two years ago. But with Stone she felt safe.

"Yes, you can leave me with something to think about," she finally said softly, after gathering her courage for whatever was to come. She didn't have long to wait to find out.

He reached out and cupped her chin in his hand, letting her know his intent and giving her every opportunity to put a stop to what he was about to do if that was what she wanted. When she didn't move or say anything, but continued to meet his gaze, while her breathing became just as erratic as his, he lowered his head to hers.

Madison felt the pull of her insides the moment their mouths touched, and immediately she felt the heat of his skin as his jeans-clad thigh brushed against her when he brought her closer into his arms. And when he settled his hands at her hips, and with it came the deep, compelling sizzle of desire, she thought she was certainly going to lose it.

Nothing prepared her for the onslaught of emotions that rammed through her when her lips parted and he entered her mouth and proceeded to kiss her in a way she had never been kissed before. It was a gentle kiss. It was tender. But on the flip side, it contained a hunger that made the pressure she felt in her chest too intense, almost unbearable.

And when he deepened the kiss, capturing her tongue with his, she was grateful that he had the mind to hold her tighter because she would surely have melted to the floor. She savored the hot sweetness of his mouth as he carried her to a level where sophistication, poise and what was proper had no place. As their tongues mingled, dueled and mated, feelings and emotions she had never felt before clashed into her, smothering her in a sexuality she hadn't known existed.

And when he finally broke the kiss, she drew in a long shuddering breath and gazed up at him. His eyes were intense and she knew that she and Stone had shared more than just a kiss. They had also shared an understanding. What was happening between them was probably no different than what his uncle and her mother had experienced.

Instant attraction.

The kind that hit two people from the first so you were compelled to do the unthinkable and act on it.

She sighed deeply and unconsciously licked her lips, tasting the dampness, a lingering reminder of his taste. Sharp coils of desire raced through her and she knew that Stone Westmoreland was a dangerous man. He was dangerous to her common sense. Although she needed to talk to Durango, she couldn't do it today. She needed time to clear her mind and think straight. At the moment the only thing she could think about was romancing Stone. In less than twenty-four hours he had unearthed another side of her, a side even she hadn't known existed and the thought of that frightened her somewhat.

"I don't think joining you and Durango this evening for dinner would be a good idea, Stone," she decided to say.

No matter how desperately she needed to know about her mother and their uncle, she also needed space from this man who caused emotions to grip her that were so foreign and unfamiliar. "I want to get settled in here first and think about a few things. Is there any way we can meet tomorrow, possibly before noon? I'd like to try and contact my mother to let her know that I'm here."

Stone held her gaze. "Tomorrow's fine, Madison. Just tell the lady at the front desk to phone Durango's ranch. They have the number and I'll be glad to come and pick you up."

"All right."

He stared at her for a few minutes then, without saying anything else, he turned and walked out of the door.

Pushing back from the kitchen table, Stone stood to help Durango clear the dishes. "I tell you, Stone, it was the strangest thing seeing Uncle Corey act that way, like a love-smitten twenty-year-old. And I didn't want to say anything in front of Madison, but her mother wasn't acting any better, although it would be clear to anyone that she was a lady with a lot of class."

Stone shook his head. "Well, Madison is determined to

find answers. I think I gave her food for thought earlier and she's pretty much accepted the idea that her mother and Uncle Corey are involved in an affair, but she still needs to understand why."

Durango raised a brow as he leaned against the table. "What's there to understand? Lust is lust."

Stone rolled his eyes upward. Durango definitely had a way with words. "Well, with her mother being such a classy, well-bred lady and all, lust as you see it is something Madison just can't seem to understand."

Durango grinned. "Then I guess it's going to be up to you to explain it all to her then. Now if you need my help in—"

"Don't even think about it," Stone responded quickly in a growl.

Durango chuckled. "Hey, I was just kidding. Besides, you know how I feel about city women anyway." Even with the laughter in his voice, his words echoed with bitterness.

Unfortunately Stone did know how he felt. "Need help with the dishes?" he asked after walking across the kitchen and placing them on the counter.

"Nope, that's what dishwashers are for. If you want we can try reaching Uncle Corey again, but take my word for it, it'll be a waste of time. He and his lady friend aren't accepting calls. I truly believe they turned the damn thing off."

Stone decided to try calling anyway and hung up later when he didn't get an answer. He shook his head emphatically. "You would think Madison's mother would have tried to reach her daughter."

Durango raised a brow. "I thought she had. Didn't Madison say on the drive over to the Silver Arrow that her mother had called to say she was fine and was extending her vacation for two weeks?"

"Yes, but she left the message on the answering machine. I'd think she would have made a point to talk to Madison directly to allay her fears."

Durango raised his eyes heavenward. "And I'd think—which is probably the same way Madison's mother is thinking—that at fifty years of age she doesn't have to check in with anyone, not even a daughter, especially if she's assured her daughter that she's okay." He grabbed an apple out of the basket and bit into it like he hadn't just eaten dinner. "Do you know what I think, Stone?"

Stone shrugged, almost too afraid to ask. "No, Durango, what do you think?"

"I think the reason Madison is so busy sticking her nose into her mother's love life…or lust life, is because she doesn't have one of her own."

A hint of a smile played at the corners of Stone's lips. "She doesn't have what? A love life or a lust life?"

"Neither of either. And I think that's where you need to step in."

Stone crossed his arms over his chest and met his cousin's direct gaze. "And do what exactly?"

Durango smiled. "Give the lady a taste of both."

Stone snorted. Only someone like Durango who had a jaded perception of love and marriage would think that way. Although Stone didn't have plans to ever settle down and marry, he did believe in love. His parents' marriage was a prime example of it, so was his sister Delaney's and his brothers Dare's and Thorn's marriages.

"I think I'm going to spend a few hours in your hot tub if you don't mind," he said to Durango.

"By all means, help yourself."

Less than twenty minutes later, Stone was sitting comfortably in the hot tub on Durango's outside deck. A good portion of Durango's land was the site of natural hot springs and the first thing he had done after building the ranch had been to take advantage of that fact and erect his own private hot tub. It was large enough to hold at least five people and the heat of the water felt good as it stimulated Stone's muscles.

He closed his eyes and immediately had thoughts of Madison. Maybe Durango was right about her failure to take her mother's words at face value that she was okay. But in just the short amount of time he had gotten to know Madison he could tell she was a person who cared deeply about those she loved. She probably couldn't help being a consummate worrier. And then maybe Durango was right again. Perhaps Madison needed something or someone in her life to occupy her time so she could stop worrying about her mother.

Stone inhaled deeply. For all he knew she might very well have someone already, some man back in Boston. He immediately pushed that thought from his mind. Madison Winters was not the type of woman who would belong to one man and willingly kiss another. And she had kissed him. Boy, had she kissed him. And he had definitely kissed her. The effects of their kiss still lingered with him. Even now he could still taste her. Durango's beef stew hadn't been strong enough to eradicate her taste from his mouth.

"Hey, Stone, you just got a call."

Stone cocked one eye open and looked at Durango who was standing a few feet away with a cold bottle of beer in his hand. "Who was it?"

"Your city girl."

Stone quickly opened both eyes and leaned forward, knowing just whom Durango was talking about. "Did she say what she wanted?"

Durango leaned against the door with a smirky grin on his face. "No, but I got the distinct impression that she wanted you."

Madison nervously paced her cabin as she waited for Stone to return her call. Deciding she had walked the floor enough, she dropped down into the nearest chair as she recounted in her mind what Frank, the husband of a good friend of hers who owned an investigative firm, had shared with her less than an hour ago. In addition to that, she couldn't help but replay back in her mind the communication she had picked up from her mother when Madison called her apartment in Boston to replay her messages.

She jumped when she heard a knock at her door and wondered who it might be. It was late and she would think most of the guests and workers at the ranch had pretty much retired for the night. She had to remember this wasn't Boston and that she was practically alone in an area where the population was sparse.

She eased her way to the door. "Who is it?"

"It's me, Madison. Stone."

She let out a sigh of relief when she heard the familiar sound of Stone's voice and quickly opened the door. "Stone, I was waiting for your call. I didn't expect you to come over here," she said, taking a step back to let him in. She was glad that, although she had showered earlier, she had slipped into a long, flowing caftan that was suitable for accepting company.

Stone entered and closed the door behind him. "Durango said you sounded upset when you called so I thought I'd come over right away." His gaze took in her features. They appeared tense and worried. "What's wrong, Madison?"

She inhaled deeply and nervously rubbed her hands together. "I don't know where to start."

Stone studied her for a moment, concerned. "Start anywhere you like. How about if we take a seat over there and you can tell me what's going on," he suggested in a calming voice.

She nodded and crossed the room to sit on the edge of the bed while he sat across from her in a wingback chair. "All right, now tell me what's wrong," he said, his tone soothing.

Madison folded her hands in her lap. A part of her was grateful to Stone for coming instead of calling, although she hadn't expected him to. She lifted her chin and met his gaze; again, like before, she felt that powerful current pass through them and wondered if he'd felt it, too.

She put the thought of the sexual chemistry that was sizzling between them to the back of her mind and started talking. "I called my apartment in Boston to retrieve my phone messages and discovered that my mother had called and left another one."

Stone lifted a dark brow. "Really? And what did she say?"

Madison sighed. "She said she regretted that we keep missing each other but that she wanted to let me know she was doing fine and…"

Stone waited for her to finish and when she seemed hesitant to do so he prodded. "And?"

Madison inhaled deeply once again before saying, "And she plans to extend her trip by an additional two weeks."

For a moment there was not a sound in the room, just this long pregnant silence. Then Stone slowly nodded as he continued to study her. He could tell the message had been upsetting to Madison. "Well, at least you know that she's okay."

Madison shook her head and Stone watch as her hair swirled around her shoulders with the movement. "No, I don't know that, Stone. I'm more worried about her than ever. There's something else I think you should know."

Stone gazed across the few feet separating them. "What?"

Madison slowly stood then nervously paced the room a few times before coming back to stand in front of Stone. "I know that you and Durango tried to reassure me that your uncle is a decent man—honest, trustworthy and safe—but I had to be sure. I had to find out everything I could about him to help me understand why my mother is behaving the way she is. A friend of mine, another teacher at the school where I work, well, her husband owns an investigation firm. After you left here today, I contacted him and gave him your uncle's name."

Stone sat back in the chair, his gaze locked with hers as he rubbed his chin. "And?"

Madison swallowed nervously. "And, according to Frank, when he entered your uncle's name into the database, he discovered another investigative firm, one that's located somewhere in Texas, was checking out your uncle's past, as well. For some reason it seems that I'm not the only one who wants information about him."

Stone frowned and sat up straight in his chair. Anger suddenly lined his features. "Are you trying to accuse my uncle of—"

"No! I'm not accusing him of anything. Even Frank indicated that he's clean and doesn't have a criminal record or anything. I just thought it was strange and felt that you should know."

Stone stared at Madison for a long moment then stood in front of her. "I don't know what interest another investigative company has in my uncle but, whatever the reason, it has nothing to do with his character, Madison. Corey Westmoreland is one of the finest men I know. I admit he can be somewhat ornery at times and set in his ways, but I would and do trust him with my life."

Madison heard the defensive anger in Stone's voice although he tried to control it. She crossed her arms over her chest and gazed up at him. "I wasn't insinuating that he wasn't a—"

"Weren't you? I also think that until you talk to your mother and see her for yourself to make sure she's not up there with some crazy mountain man, you won't have a moment of peace."

Unable to help himself, Stone reached out and brushed a strand of hair back from her face. There were tension lines around her eyes and the mouth he had kissed earlier that day was strained, agitated and on edge. "And I intend to give you that peace. I will take you up Corey's Mountain myself."

His words had an immediate effect on Madison and she

released her arms from across her chest. Her heart began beating a mile a minute. "You will?" she asked in a rush.

"Yes. I would head up there first thing in the morning, but unfortunately you don't have the proper attire to make such a trip. We need to take care of that as well as getting the supplies we'll need. If all that works out then we can leave the day after tomorrow, bright and early. We'll take a truck as far as Martin Quinns' ranch, then borrow a couple of his horses to go the rest of the way on up."

Madison tried to mask her relief. She hated admitting it but Stone was right. She wouldn't have a moment of peace until she saw and talked to her mother herself. "I'll make sure I get all the things I need."

Stone nodded. "I'm going to make sure you get all the things you need, too. I'll be picking you up in the morning to drive you into town and take you to the general store. We should be able to purchase everything we'll need from there."

Madison nodded. Uncertain what to say next she knew of the one thing that she *had* to say. "Thank you, Stone."

Her heart lurched in her chest when she saw that her words of thanks had not softened the lines around his eyes. He was still upset with her for what she'd insinuated about his uncle.

"Don't mention it. I'll see you in the morning." And without saying anything else, he crossed the room and walked out of the door.

Four

Whoever said you can take the girl out of the city but you can't take the city out of the girl must have known a woman like Madison Winters, Stone thought, as he sat silently in the chair with his long legs stretched out in front of him and watched her move around the cabin packing for their trip.

That morning they had gone to the general store to purchase the items they would need. Getting her prepared for their excursion had taken up more time than he figured it would. When he had inventoried what she'd brought with her from Boston, he hadn't been surprised to discover her stylish clothing—mostly with designer labels—included nothing that would be durable enough to travel up into the mountains. When they'd driven into town she had agreed with his suggestion that she buy several pairs of jeans, T-shirts, flannel shirts, a couple of sweaters, a wool jacket, heavy-duty socks and, most important, good hiking boots. He had also strongly suggested that she buy a wide-brimmed hat. He'd explained to her that the days would be hot and the nights would be cold.

He had taken care of the other things such as the food they would need, the sleeping bags they would use, as well as the rental of the truck that would carry them as far as the Quinns' ranch.

Stone's lips broke into an innately male smile as he continued to watch her. She was definitely a gorgeous woman but, more than that, he found her downright fasci-nating. He would even go so far as to say that she intrigued him, especially now when she was frowning while glanc-ing down at herself, as if the thought of wearing jeans and a flannel shirt was nothing she would ever get used to.

Hell, it was something he doubted he would get used to, either. He had seen plenty of women in jeans in his life-time but none, and he meant none, could wear them like they'd been exclusively designed just for their bodies. An-other man might say that she was built and had everything in all the right places, but the writer in him would go fur-ther than that and say she was…*a summer pleasure and a fall treasure whose beauty was as breathtaking and capti-vating as a cluster of tulips and daffodils under a spectac-ular Montana sky.*

"Do you think I packed enough, Stone?"

Her words intruded on his musings and he glanced at the bed. To be quite honest she had packed too much, but he knew that was the norm for any woman. Somehow they would manage even if it meant leaving some of it at the Quinns' ranch once they got there. The back of a horse could handle only so much on what would be a treacherous climb up the mountain.

"No, you're fine," he said coming to his feet. "I contacted Martin Quinn and he's expecting us by noon tomorrow. We'll sleep overnight at his place then head up the mountain right after breakfast. If our timing is right, we won't have to spend but one night out under the stars."

Madison raised a brow. "It will take us two days to get to your uncle's ranch?"

"Yes, by horseback. At some point during the daylight hours it will be too hot to travel and we'll need to give the horses periodic breaks."

Madison nodded. She then cleared her throat. "Stone, I want to thank you for—"

"You've thanked me already," he said, picking up the Stetson that he had purchased that day off the table.

"Yes, I know, but I also know that taking me to your uncle's place is intruding into your writing time."

He looked at her and the liquid heat that had started flowing through his bloodstream from the moment he had met her was still there. "No, you're not," he said, forcing himself to ignore how good she smelled. "I had planned to go visit Uncle Corey anyway while I was here, so now is just as good a time as any."

"Oh, I see."

Stone doubted that she saw anything. If she did she would have second thoughts of them spending so much time together over the next three days. If she really had her eyes wide-open she would see that he wanted her with a passion so thick he could cut it with a knife. The clean scent of the mountains had nothing on her. She had a fragrance all her own and it was one that reminded him of everything a woman was supposed to be. She was more than just a city girl. She was sensuality on legs and a gorgeous pair of them at that.

He couldn't believe it had only been yesterday when he had first looked into eyes that were so mesmerizing they had taken his breath away. And since then, undercurrents of sensual tension had surrounded them whenever they were together, leaving them no slack but a whole lot of close encounters of the lush kind. He had never been this incredibly aware of a woman in his life.

"Well, I guess that's it until tomorrow morning."

Her words cut into his thoughts, reminding him that he had stood to leave yet hadn't moved an inch. "Yes, I think that's about it except for your attitude about things."

She lifted her chin just a bit. "What do you mean?"

He rather liked to see whenever she became irritated about something. She became even sexier. "I mean," he began slowly, deciding that no matter how sexy she got when she was mad, he didn't want to get her pissed off too much. "Before we head up toward Uncle Corey's mountain, you need to come to terms with what we might find when we get there, Madison."

He watched as she averted her eyes from his briefly and he knew she understood exactly what he meant. She tilted her head and their gazes connected again. "I hear what you're saying but I don't know if I can, Stone. She's my mother," she said quietly.

Stone held her gaze intently. Logical thinking—which he knew she wasn't exemplifying at the moment—dictated that he have something to say to that. So he did.

"She's also a full-grown woman who's old enough to make her own decisions."

She sighed and he could just feel the varied emotions tumbling through her. "But she's never done anything like this before."

"There's a first time for everything." He of all people should know that. Until yesterday, no woman had taken hold of his senses the way she had. He wasn't exactly happy about it and in some ways he found it downright disturbing. But he was mature enough to accept it as the way things happen sometimes between a man and a woman. Unlike his brother Thorn who liked challenges, he was one of those men who tried looking at things logically without complications and definitely without a whole lot of fuss. He accepted things easily and knew how to roll with the flow.

Madison was a very desirable woman and he was a hot-blooded male. He had conceded from the first that getting together with her would be like pouring kerosene on a fire. The end result—total combustion. The only problem with that picture was that, no matter how hot they could burn up the sheets, on some things he had made up his mind with no chance of changing it. Getting involved in a permanent relationship with a woman was one of them. It wouldn't happen.

Seeing the look of uncertainty on her face, he knew she was a long way from accepting the possibility that her mother and his uncle were lovers. As strange as it seemed, he had come to terms with it and eventually she would have to do the same. "I suggest that you get a good night's sleep," he said, moving toward the door. He intended to open it and walk out without looking back.

But he couldn't.

He turned and reached out and pulled her to him, encircling her waist and resting her head on his chest. Some inner part of him just knew that she needed to be held in his embrace. And that same inner part of him also knew that she needed a kiss, as well.

A tenderness fed by a burning flame of desire raced through him, making his heartbeat quicken and his body go hard. She must have felt his arousal and lifted her head. Their gazes locked. Words weren't needed, sexual chemistry had a language all its own and it was speaking to them loud and clear.

She parted her lips on a sigh and he lowered his head and captured the very essence of that moan with his mouth. The taste of her was tempting, and he immediately thought of silken sheets, burning candles and soft music. He thought of touching her all over, loving her with his mouth and his hands until she groaned out his name, then placing her beneath him, entering her, thrusting in and out in the same rhythm he was using at that very moment on her mouth. All during the previous night he'd had a hard time sleeping because his body had silently yearned for her. And he knew tonight, tomorrow night and all of the nights after that wouldn't be any different.

After a long moment, he broke off the kiss and rested his forehead against hers. Kissing her was exhausting as well as stimulating. He could have continued kissing her forever if he hadn't needed to breathe.

"Stone?"

He inhaled and tried to get his body to relax, but her scent filled his nostrils making regaining his calm downright difficult. "Yeah?"

"This isn't good is it?"

He chuckled against her ear. "You don't hear me complaining, Madison."

"You know what I mean."

Yes, he knew exactly what she meant. "If I go along with your way of thinking, that we should place our full concentration on your mother and Uncle Corey and not on each other, then I would have to agree that it isn't good because the timing is lousy. But if I adhere to my own thoughts, that I feel whatever is going on between my uncle and your mother is their business and that you and I should place our full concentration on each other, then I would say it is good."

He said the words while a barrage of emotions raced through him. They were emotions he wasn't used to dealing with. A part of him suddenly felt disoriented. Totally confused. Fully aware.

The woman he held in his arms was as intoxicating as the most potent brand of whiskey and she had his senses reeling and his body heated. "I'm going to leave the decision as to how we should handle things up to you, Madison. I suggest you sleep on it and let me know what you decide in the morning."

Leaning down, he kissed her again; this kiss was tender but just as passionate as the one before. He pulled back and released her, opened the door and walked out into the cool Montana night.

Clinging to the strength of the decisions she had made overnight, Madison opened the door for Stone the next morning. The eyes that met hers were sharp, direct and she immediately felt herself wavering on one decision in particular as she inwardly asked herself: *how can I stand behind my decision to make sure that nothing happens between us?*

Of the two decisions she'd made, that had been the hardest one and, as she glanced at the strong, vital and sexy man standing in the doorway, she knew it would be the hardest one to keep. Stone wasn't a man any woman could ignore and being alone with him for the next few days would definitely test her resolve. If she were smart she would put any thoughts of a relationship between them out of her mind completely. She had never been involved in any sort of casual affair before and wasn't sure that type of relationship would suit her. But then she had to remember that she had thought her relationship with Cedric had been anything but casual and look where it had gotten her.

"You're earlier than I expected," she somehow found her voice to say. In the predawn light that encompassed him, she searched his eyes for any signs of decisions that he himself might have made and only saw the heated look of desire that had been there from the very first. And she knew if she was ever undisciplined enough to risk all and take a chance, this man would and could introduce her to passion of the hottest kind.

He was standing before her so utterly handsome in his jeans, flannel shirt, boots and Stetson. He looked nothing like an action-thriller author but everything like a rugged cowboy who made the unspoiled land surrounding Montana's Rocky Mountains his home. But she knew there was something else about him that was holding her interest. It was what she saw beyond the clothes. It was the man himself. There was a depth to him that was greater than any man she'd ever met. There was a self-confidence about him that had nothing to do with arrogance and a kindness that had nothing to do with a sense of duty. He did things out of the generosity of his heart and concern for others and not for show. And she felt loyalty to him. He would be true to whatever woman he claimed as his. Cedric could certainly have taken a few lessons from Stone Westmoreland.

He smiled. "I thought we could grab something to eat on the way," he said, interrupting her thoughts. She sighed, grateful that he had. She could have stood there and stacked up all his strong points all day.

She offered him a smile. A part of her was tempted to offer a lot more. He had just that sort of effect on her. "All right. I just need to grab my luggage."

"I'll get it," he said, entering her cabin, immediately filling the space with his heat and making her totally aware of him, even more than she had been before. She watched as he glanced over at the luggage she had neatly lined up next to her bed. Then he looked at her and she heard him swear under his breath before moving—not toward the luggage but toward her.

"I don't know what decisions you made about us," he said in a low, husky voice. "But I thought of you all last night and I swore that as soon as I saw you this morning I would do something."

"What?" she asked, trying to ignore the seductive scent of his aftershave as well as the intense beating of her heart.

"Taste you."

Madison's breath caught and, before she could release a sigh, Stone captured her mouth in his. As soon as their tongues touched she knew she would remember every sweet and tantalizing thing about his kiss. Especially the way his tongue was dueling with hers, staking a claim she didn't want him to have but one he was taking anyway as he tried kissing the taste right out of her mouth. His tongue was dominating, it was bold and it left no doubt in her mind that when it came to kissing, Stone was an ace, a master, a perfectionist. She placed her arms around his neck, more to stop from melting at his feet than for support. He had a way of making her feel sexy, feminine and desirable; something Cedric had never done.

Moments later, when he broke off the kiss and slowly lifted his head to look down at her, she couldn't help asking, "Got enough?"

"Not by a long shot," he said hotly against her moist lips. Then he leaned down and kissed her again and Madison quickly decided, what the heck. Once she had told him of her decision about them he wouldn't be kissing her again anytime soon, so she would gladly take what she could for now.

Her common sense tried kicking in—although it didn't have the punch to force her to pull from his arms just yet. Her practical side was reminding her that she'd only met Stone two days ago. Her passionate side countered that bit of logic with the fact that in those two days she probably knew him a lot better than she'd known Cedric in the three years they had dated. Stone was everything her former fiancé was not—including one hell of a kisser.

Desire surged through her and she knew if she didn't pull back now the unthinkable might happen. But then a rebel part of her that barely ever surfaced hinted that the unthinkable in this case just might be something she should do.

She didn't have much time to think about it further when Stone lifted his mouth again and she, regretfully, released her arms from around his neck and took a step back, putting space between them.

"I guess I better grab that luggage so we can leave," he said, keeping his gaze glued to her face.

"That's a good idea and I don't think there should be any more physical contact between us until we talk," she said softly, trying to hold on to the resolve she'd had that morning. The same resolve his kiss had almost swiped from her.

She watched as he arched a dark brow. "You've made decisions?"

Her gaze held on to his. "Yes."

He nodded then walked across the room for her luggage.

"Tell me about yourself, Stone, and I would love hearing about all of your books."

Stone briefly glanced across the seat of the truck and met Madison's inquiring gaze. They had been on the road for over an hour already and she'd yet to tell him of any decisions she'd made. Even when they had stopped at a café for breakfast she hadn't brought their relationship up. Instead she had talked about how beautiful the land was, how much she had enjoyed teaching last year and about a trip to Paris she had taken last month. She was stalling. He knew it and knew that she knew it, as well.

"Do you want to know about Stone Westmoreland or about Rock Mason?"

A bemused frown touched her face. "Aren't they one and the same?"

"No. To the people I know I'm Stone Westmoreland. To

my readers, the majority of whom don't know me, I'm Rock Mason—a name I made up to protect my privacy. I should correct that and say it's a name my sister Delaney came up with. At the time she was eighteen and thought it sounded cool."

She nodded. "And which one of those individuals are you now?"

"Stone."

She nodded again. And although she had made her mind up not to go there, she couldn't help but ask. The need to know was too strong. "And each of the times you kissed me, who were you?"

He glanced over at her. "Stone." He then pulled off the road, stopped the car and turned to her. "Maybe I need to explain things, Madison. I don't have a split personality. I'm merely saying that a lot of people read a book a person writes and assume they know that individual just because of the words he or she puts on paper. But there's more to me than what is between the pages of my novels. I write to entertain. I enjoy doing so and it pays the bills in a real nice way. Whenever I finish a book I feel a sense of accomplishment and achievement. But when all is said and done, I'm still a normal human being—a man who has strong values and convictions about certain things. I'm a man who's proud to be an African-American and I'm someone who loves his family. I have my work and I have my privacy. For my work I am Rock Mason and for my private life I am Stone. I consider you as part of my private life." With that said he started the car and pulled back on the main road.

Madison blew out a breath. The very thought that he considered her part of his life at all made her heart pound and parts of her feel soft and gooey inside. "So tell me something about the private life of Stone Westmoreland."

Her request drew his brows together as he remembered the last time a woman had asked him that. Noreen Baker, an entertainment reporter who'd wanted to do an interview on him for *Today's Man* magazine. The woman had been attractive but pushy as hell. He hadn't liked her style and had decided when she'd tried delving into his personal life that he hadn't liked her. But she was determined not to be deterred and had decided one way or another she would get her story.

She never got her story and found out the hard way that, although on any given day he was typically pretty nice and easygoing, when pissed off he could be hell to deal with. Instead of giving her the exclusive she had desired, he had agreed to let someone else do a story on him.

"I'm thirty-three, closer to thirty-four with a birthday coming up in August, single, and have never been married and don't plan on ever getting married."

Madison lifted a brow. "Why?"

"It's the accountability factor. I love being single. I like coming and going whenever I please and, with being a writer, I need the freedom of going places to do research, book signings, to clear my mind, relax and to be just plain lazy when I want to. I'm not responsible for anyone other than myself and I like it that way." He decided not to tell her that another reason he planned to stay single was that he saw marriage as giving up control of his life and giving more time to a wife than to his writing.

Madison nodded. "So there's not a special person in your life?"

"No." But then he thought she was special and he had pretty much accepted that she was in his life…at least at the present time.

"What about your immediate family?"

"My parents are still living and doing well. My father works with the construction company my grandfather started years ago. He's a twin."

Madison had shifted her body in the seat to search her pockets for a piece of chewing gum and glanced over at Stone. "Who's a twin?"

"My father. As well as my two brothers, Chase and Storm, and my cousins, Ian and Quade. They are Durango's brothers."

"Are they all identical twins?" she asked fascinated. She'd never heard of so many multiple births in one family before.

"No, everyone is fraternal, thank God. I can't imagine two of Storm. He can be a handful and considers himself a ladies' man."

Madison smiled, hearing the affection in his voice. "How many brothers do you have?"

"Four brothers and one sister. Delaney, who we call Laney, is the baby."

Madison frowned. "Delaney Westmoreland? Now where have I heard that name before?"

Stone chuckled. "Probably read about her. *People* magazine did a spread on her almost a year and a half ago when she married a prince from the Middle East by the name of Jamal Ari Yasir."

A huge smile touched Madison's face. "That's right, I remember reading that article. *Essence* magazine did an article on her, as well. Wow! I remember reading it during…"

Stone glanced over at her to see why she hadn't finished what she was about to say. Her smile was no longer there. "During what?"

She met his gaze briefly before he returned it to the road. "During the time I broke up with my fiancé. It was good reading something as warm, loving and special as the story about your sister and her prince; especially after finding out what a toad my own fiancé was."

"What did he do?"

Madison glanced down at her hands that were folded in her lap before glancing over at Stone. His eyes were on the road but she knew that she had his complete attention and was waiting for her response. "I found out right before our wedding that he'd been having an affair. He came up with a lot of reasons why he did it, but none were acceptable."

"Hell, I should hope not," Stone said with more than a hint of anger in his voice. "The man was a fool."

"And she was a model."

Stone lifted a brow. "Who?"

"The woman he was sleeping with. He said that that justified his behavior. He believed he was actually using her so as not to wear me down. He wanted to preserve me for later."

A dark frown covered Stone's face. "He actually said that?"

"Yes. Cedric was quite a character."

Stone didn't want to get too personal, but he couldn't help asking, "So the two of you never, ahh, never slept together?"

Instead of looking over at him he watched as she quickly

glanced out the window. "Yes, we did but just twice during the two years we were together."

Stone shook his head. "Like I said before, he was a fool."

Madison leaned back comfortably in her seat. She was glad Stone felt that way. Cedric had tried to convince her that just because he'd been involved in one affair was no reason to call off their wedding. A model, he'd tried to explain, was every man's fantasy girl. That didn't mean he had loved her less, it only meant he was fulfilling one of his fantasies. She guessed fulfillment of fantasies came before fidelity.

"Tell me some more about you, Stone," she said, not wanting to think anymore about Cedric and the pain he had caused her.

She listened for the next few miles while Stone continued to tell her about his family. He talked about his brother Dare who was a sheriff and Chase who owned a restaurant in downtown Atlanta. Once again she was surprised to discover that he had another well-known sibling—Thorn Westmoreland, the motorcycle builder and racer who had won the big bike race in Daytona earlier that year.

"I've seen your brother's bikes and they're beautiful. He's very skillful."

"Yes, he is," he said. "He got married last month and is in the process of teaching his wife how to handle a bike."

By the time they had reached the Quinns' ranch, Madison felt she knew a good bit about Stone. He had openly shared things about himself and the people he cared about. She knew he never, ever wanted to marry but was proud that his parents' marriage had lasted for such a long time. And he was genuinely happy for his sister and brothers and their marriages.

When they pulled the truck up in front of the sprawling ranch house, Madison caught her breath. It was breathtaking and like nothing she had ever seen before. "This place is beautiful," she said when Stone opened the truck door for her to get out.

He laughed. "If you think this place leaves you gasping for air, just wait until you see Uncle Corey's place. Now that place is a work of art."

Madison couldn't wait to see it. Nor could she wait to see her mother. Stone must have read the look in her eyes because he gently squeezed her hand in his, giving her assurance. "She's fine and you'll see her soon enough."

She nodded. Thankful. Before she could say anything a woman, who appeared to be in her middle fifties, came out the front door of the house with a huge smile on her face. She was beautiful and it was quite obvious she was Native American. Her dark eyes were huge in her angular face. She had high cheekbones and long, straight black hair that flowed down her back. "Why, if it isn't Stone Westmoreland. Martin said you were coming and I decided to cook an apple pie for the occasion. I'll share if you autograph a few books for me."

Stone laughed as he swept the woman off her feet into his arms for a hug. "Anything for you, Mrs. Quinn. And you know how much I love your apple pie." When he had placed her back on her feet he turned her around so he could introduce her to Madison.

"Madison, this is Morning Star Quinn, Martin's wife. They are good friends of my uncle Corey and their son McKinnon is Durango's best friend."

Madison smiled. It was easy to see that the woman had

Stone's affection and respect. She offered Morning Star Quinn her hand to shake, liking her on the spot. She seemed like such a vibrant person who blended in well with her surroundings. "It's nice meeting you."

"It's nice meeting you, as well. And I've prepared a place for the two of you to stay overnight. I understand you are on your way up to see Corey."

Stone nodded. "Yes. Mr. Quinn mentioned when I spoke with him on the phone yesterday that the two of you haven't seen Uncle Corey in a while."

Morning Star Quinn shook her head. "It's been weeks. He's missed the Thursday night poker game for almost three weeks now, and you know for your uncle that's unusual. But we know he's all right."

"How do you know that for certain?" Madison couldn't help but ask.

Morning Star Quinn raised a curious brow as if wondering why she was interested then smiled at her and responded. "He came down off the mountain a couple of days ago to use the phone. It seems something is wrong with his telephone, which is the reason no one has heard from him. Martin and I had gone to town so we didn't get a chance to see him, but McKinnon was here and had a chance to talk to him. He assured us that Corey was fine."

Mrs. Quinn then switched her gaze to Stone. "McKinnon also said he had a woman with him; a very nice-looking woman at that. Of course that surprised all of us because you know how Corey feels about a woman being on his mountain."

Stone shook his head, smiling. "Yes, I know. In fact that's one of the reasons we're going up to see him."

Tapping her finger to her bottom lip, Morning Star Quinn gazed thoughtfully at Stone. "Then you know her? You know who this woman is?"

Madison knew that, out of consideration for her mother's reputation, Stone would not say. But she knew that Morning Star Quinn was a person that she could be honest with; and was a person that she *wanted* to be honest with. "Yes, we know who she is," Madison finally answered. "The woman up there on the mountain with Corey Westmoreland is my mother."

Four

Nothing, Madison thought as she walked outside on the huge porch, could be more beautiful than a night under a Montana sky. Even in darkness she could see the outlines of the Rockies looming in the background and was starkly amazed at just how vastly different this place was from Boston.

She turned when she heard the door open behind her and wasn't surprised to see it was Stone. She smiled as she took a couple of minutes to calm the rapid beating of her heart. The more time she spent with him, the more she appreciated him as a man…a very considerate and caring man. Even now she could feel the warmth of his eyes touching her.

Earlier he had helped her unload her luggage and had placed it in the bedroom that Mrs. Quinn had given her to use. Then later, after she had gotten settled, he had come for her when Martin Quinn and his son McKinnon had come home. She had blinked twice when she saw McKinnon. The man was simply gorgeous and had inherited his mother's golden complexion. After introductions had been made, Stone had asked her to take a walk with him to show her around the Quinns' ranch before dinnertime.

On their stroll, he had shared stories with her about how, while growing up, he and his brothers and cousins would visit this area every summer to spend time with their Uncle Corey. It was a guy thing, which meant Delaney was never included in those summer retreats. She usually came to Montana during her school's spring breaks. Stone also shared with her the little escapades the eleven Westmoreland boys and McKinnon and his three brothers had gotten into. He had made her smile, chuckle and even laugh a few times, and for a little while she had forgotten the reason she had come to Montana in the first place. At dinner she had met Morning Star and Martin's other three sons, who were younger than McKinnon, but who had also inherited their mother's Blackfoot coloring, instead of the light complexion of their Caucasian father.

"You okay?" Stone asked quietly, coming to stand beside her.

She tipped her head to look up at him. When he placed his arms around her shoulders as if to ward off the chill in the air, she became very aware of how male he was. And the nice thing about it was that he didn't flaunt it. In fact he seemed totally unaware of the sensuality oozing from him. "Yes, I'm fine. Dinner was wonderful, wasn't it?"

"Yes. Mrs. Quinn always knew how to cook and her apple pie has always been my favorite," he answered.

Madison grinned when she remembered the number of slices he'd eaten and said, "Yeah, I could tell." She then thought of something. "They didn't say a lot about your uncle at dinner." She felt his fingers inch upward to caress the side of her neck, sending a glimmer of heat through her.

"There wasn't much to say. They know the man Uncle Corey is and know that your mother isn't in any danger."

She shot him a quick look. "I know she isn't in any danger with him, Stone. I just don't understand what's going on. And I'm beginning to understand a bit about instant attraction if that's what it was, but still I have to talk to her anyway."

"I understand," he said, giving her shoulders a quick squeeze.

A part of Madison wondered if he did understand when there were times when she didn't.

"Tell me about your parents, Madison."

His question caught her off guard. "My parents?"

"Yes. What sort of marriage did they have?"

She frowned, not sure why he was asking and whether or not she was willing to disclose any details of her parents' relationship as she had seen it. But this was Stone. He had stopped being a stranger to her that first day on the plane and she figured there must be a reason that he wanted to know. "It was nothing like the Quinns' marriage, that's for sure," she said in a rush.

The sound of his chuckle filled the night air. "It wasn't?"

She leaned back and looked up at him as she thought of the two adults with four grown sons. Even with visitors sitting at the dinner table with their sons, they still exchanged smiles filled with over thirty years of intimacies. "No, it wasn't. Is your parents' marriage like theirs?"

Stone looked down at her and she could actually see the smile that touched both corners of his mouth. "Umm, pretty much. I'm proud of the fact that my parents have shared a long marriage, but even prouder that they are still very much in love after nearly forty years."

He shifted his body to lean against the porch rail and took her with him, letting her hip rest along the strength of his. "They claim it was love at first sight after meeting one weekend at a church function. Within two weeks they were married."

He decided not to tell her that his parents' had predicted that their six children would also find love that way—at first sight. So far Delaney claimed that's how it had been for her and Jamal, although realizing it had been the tough part for her, as well as for Jamal. And everyone knew the moment Dare had gotten zapped. Stone and Shelly were friends in high school and working on a project together when Dare had come home unexpectedly from college and walked into the living room. He had taken one look at the sixteen-year-old Shelly Brockman and fallen in love with her then and there.

Then there was Thorn. Tara had been his challenge, as well as the love of his life from the moment she had stormed out of their sister Delaney's kitchen one night to give the unsuspecting Thorn hell about something. She had taken him aback and had also taken his heart in that same minute. Again, love at first sight.

He released a deep sigh. That may have been the way things had happened for his sister and two brothers but it wouldn't happen that way for him. He wouldn't let it.

"Your parents like touching, Stone?"

Madison's question interrupted Stone's thoughts and he couldn't help but chuckle again when he thought of the many times he'd seen his father playfully pat his mother on her behind. "Yes, and they also occasionally kiss in front of us. Always have. We're used to it. Nothing real passionate but enough to let anyone know that they still love each other. I'm sure they leave the heavy-duty hanky-panky stuff in the bedroom," he said grinning, not at all bothered by the fact that his parents might still have an active sex life. He pulled Madison closer to him. "Didn't your parents ever touch?"

After a brief moment she shrugged. "I'd never seen them touch. And I'd never thought anything about it until I went away for the weekend to spend some time at a friend's house. Her parents were like the Quinns…and probably a lot like your parents. It was easy to see they loved and respected each other and it suddenly hit me what was missing at my house, between my parents. Then I started watching them closely and I began to realize that, although they liked and respected each other, they were two people who were not in love but locked in a marriage anyway."

Stone lifted a brow. "Why would they stay married if they didn't love each other?"

She sighed deeply. "I can think of several reasons. Me for one. They would have stayed together just for me. I know in my heart that my parents loved me. I was my daddy's girl and my mother's daughter. I had a great relationship with them both. My father's death was hard on me."

Silence stretched between them; then she said, "Another reason they would have possibly stayed together is for religious reasons. They were both devout Catholics who didn't believe in divorce. It was til-death-do-you-part."

Stone nodded, taking in everything she'd said. "Didn't you say that your father has been dead for ten years?"

"Yes, he died when I was fifteen."

"And during that time, since his death, your mother has never been romantically involved with anyone?"

"No."

"Don't you think that's odd?"

She heaved a sigh. "I never thought about it before. I always assumed she just wanted to bury herself in her work after my father's death. I never assumed she was lonely and in need of companionship."

"Well, that might be the reason she took off with Uncle Corey. There are some things a man or woman can't control at times. Passion. Especially if they haven't shared it with anyone in a while. Hormones are known to get the best of you if you aren't careful."

Madison wondered if he was speaking from experience? She hadn't slept with anyone since Cedric and she definitely didn't feel like she was missing out on anything. He had been her first lover and she really didn't care if he was her last.

But then, standing so close to Stone with the feel of his warm breath on her cheek, she knew she had to rethink that declaration. Any time he had held her in his arms against his broad chest, her temperature had had a tendency to go up a notch. And whenever she had leaned into his aroused body while they kissed, it always amazed her that he had wanted her. And she would have to admit she had spent the last couple of nights in bed wondering how it would feel if he were to make love to her; for him to climb on top of her and—

"Are you cold, Madison?"

She was jerked out of her racy thoughts. She cleared her throat. "No, why do you ask?"

"Because you were shivering a few moments ago."

"Oh." She met his gaze when he looked down at her. She hoped he didn't have a clue as to why she had been trembling.

"What about you and your fiancé?" Stone asked, pulling her closer so that her cheek rested on his shoulder.

"What about us?"

"I know you said the two of you weren't intimate often, but did you do a lot of touching?"

She sighed deeply. There was an inner urgency within her to share with Stone how things had been with her and Cedric. She'd already told him that they had slept together only a couple of times but now he needed to hear the rest.

"Cedric and I didn't do a whole lot of anything, Stone. I mentioned earlier today that we were intimate two times, but even then it wasn't for enjoyment. It was done only to make sure we were compatible."

Stone shook his head, not sure he'd heard her right. *They'd been intimate a couple of times not for enjoyment but just to make sure they were compatible?* Now he had heard it all. How in the world could you be compatible without enjoyment? "What about passion?"

She shrugged. "What about it?"

Nothing, if you have to ask, he thought. But then he decided that he needed to appease his curiosity anyway. "Weren't there ever times when the two of you lost control?"

She chuckled as if the thought of his question was ridiculous. "No, and to be quite honest, I never experienced real physical attraction until I met you."

Damn, Stone thought. He wished she hadn't told him that mainly because it was the same way with him. He, too, had never experienced real physical attraction until he had met her. Oh, sure, he'd felt lust for a woman before but for some reason the attraction with Madison was totally different. He thought about her during some of the oddest times and, whenever he did, unexplainable warmth would flood his insides. He never, ever remembered actually hungering for a woman until he had met her. And now she was a constant craving and that didn't bode well.

After a few moments, he said, "I guess we're going to have to come up with some ground rules once we leave here and head up into the mountains."

It took Madison a moment to realize what he meant. But she decided to pretend otherwise and ask just to make sure. "Ground rules?"

"Yes, about us, Madison. About this attraction we can both honestly admit that we have for each other. About these hormones of mine that don't want to behave worth a damn. And about the fact you haven't told me what decisions you've made."

Madison forced a lump down her throat. She quickly remembered the decisions she had made overnight; the ones she'd been determined to stick to when she'd woken that morning. She knew that doing things her way was for the best.

She released a long, resigned sigh and said, "I think we should only concentrate on the situation with your uncle and my mother. At the present time my mind isn't free to dwell on anything else. I'm not sure how you may feel about it but I prefer that any thoughts about anything between us be placed on the back burner to be analyzed and discussed later, after I see my mother."

Stone shook his head. Back burner, hell! Did she think things would be that easy? Did she actually think two people could turn off sexual chemistry like it flowed from a faucet or tuck it away like an agenda item to be looked at and discussed later? Didn't she realize how difficult it would be for them once they were alone together in the mountains, in constant close proximity to each other?

No, he quickly concluded. She didn't know. She didn't have a clue because, from what he'd gathered tonight from their conversation, her parents had not been passionate beings. And, to make matters worse, her fiancé had been a damn poor excuse for a man. Instead of introducing the woman he was engaged to marry to fiery passion and red-hot desire, the bastard had been too busy doing it with a model.

A part of Stone was glad he had discovered the reason behind Madison's irrational thoughts on the situation involving his uncle and her mother. She couldn't see passion and desire for what they were if she had never experienced them before. It was obvious that she had never felt toe-curling, scream-til-your-throat-becomes-raw passion. Those sensations were something everyone should experience at some point in their lives. He couldn't imagine anything worse than having to suppress your desires—especially for a long period of time.

He quickly made a decision. He would introduce Madison to the pleasures of sex. She would soon discover that the attraction between them was something neither of them could ignore. He wanted to show her what it meant to have uncontrollable hormones zap the very sense out of you. He wouldn't do anything in particular, just sit back and let nature take its course and, considering everything, he had all the confidence in the world that it would.

Stone Westmoreland was convinced that by the time they reached his uncle's cabin, his city girl would have a clear understanding of how easy it was for a person to lose control to passion of the strongest, most potent kind.

"And you're sure that's the way you want things?" he asked after a long moment of silence.

"Yes. It will be for the best."

He nodded as a slow smile touched his lips. What Madison didn't know was that the best was yet to come. He would give her a summer night in the mountains that she would remember for a long time.

The next morning Stone glanced over at Madison as she sat patiently on her horse. He actually envied the animal's back. He would just love to have her sitting on him with her legs flanking him on both sides while she rode him to sweet oblivion.

He had not gotten much sleep last night, thinking of her and their trip up into the mountains together. He hadn't changed his mind. Before they reached his uncle's place he intended to have taught his city girl a few things. She would see how it was to deal with a real flesh-and-blood man. A man who appreciated everything a woman stood for.

He glanced up at the sky. The sun hadn't quite come up yet which meant it was a good time to start their trip. He could hardly wait. Anticipation was eating away at him, fueling his desire for her even more. "You okay?" he decided to ask her.

She smiled over at him. "Yes, I'll be fine just as long as you're not expecting an experienced cowgirl. I can do okay with a horse but, like I told you, even with the lessons I took, I'm not much of a rider."

He nodded. All that would be changing. She might not be much of a rider now but by the time they reached his uncle's cabin she would be pretty proficient at it. He would definitely teach her how to ride an animal of the two-legged kind.

"Do you think we will come across any wild animals?"

Her question made him stop what he was doing with his saddle and glance over at her. A smile tilted his lips. "You mean which kind of wild animals do you hope that we won't encounter?"

She chuckled and the sound made his stomach clench in desire. It was such a sexy sound and was like a caress to his already sensitized flesh. "Yeah, that's it."

He took the time to get on his horse before answering her. "Namely bears, wolves and mountain lions."

"Oh."

He grinned over at her when he saw the look of fear that appeared in her eyes. "Don't worry. The path I plan to take is one that's well used and most wild animals know to avoid it." He decided not to tell her that he would be taking another route that would delay their arrival at his uncle Corey's ranch by a full day. Madison Winters needed an education in wildlife of the human kind.

But first he had to get his libido under control, which wasn't easy. She looked so desirable sitting on the horse with her face tipped up to the sun. She had pulled her hair back in a ponytail and was wearing the big wide-brimmed hat on her head. But still, he could see her beautiful dark skin glowing in the predawn light. She was a natural beauty and he wondered how he would be able to keep his hands off her until she made the first move. And she would make the first move. He would see to it. He would lay temptation at her feet, then wait for her to act on it.

"Ready?" he asked, looking over at her.

"Yes."

"Okay then, let's go." They started at a slow pace since he wanted her to get the feel of the animal beneath her. He wanted her to be aware of everything around her; the way the sun was beginning to rise over the mountains, the rustle of the wind through the trees, and the sound of pine needles snapping under their horses' feet. And he wanted to make sure she was aware of him; the man who wanted her.

If she wasn't aware of it now, she would definitely be aware of it later.

They rode in silence for the first few hours, only engaging in conversation when he pointed out something of interest to her. He liked the way she appreciated her surroundings. She might be a city girl, but it was apparent she was enjoying embarking on their journey.

"Thirsty?" he asked, wondering if the ride had taken a toll on her yet. The sun had come up fully now and the heat of it was beaming down on them. He was grateful he was wearing his hat and that she had followed his suggestion and had worn hers.

"Yes, I'm thirsty."

"How about a drink of water?"

"That would be nice," she said, as he brought the horses to a stop.

"Just sit tight while I get the canteen. Mr. Quinn told me before we left that during this past year he and McKinnon built a cabin that's located halfway to Corey's place. They use it when he and his sons go hunting in these parts. He said that we could use it if we liked. So if we make it there before nightfall, we won't have to sleep outside after all."

He idly stroked the back of his horse, wishing it were Madison's body. He then added, "And there's a place up ahead where we can camp for a while and eat lunch. If we continue at this pace, we should be able to make it there before it gets much hotter."

The look on Madison's face indicated that she hoped they would. He grinned. She was being a real trooper. A lot of women would be whining and complaining by now. He remembered the first time his father had decided to take Delaney camping with him and his brothers. He shook his head at the memory. That had been the first and the last time.

He got off his horse and, after making sure both of their mounts' reins were securely tied to a nearby tree, he went to her saddlebag and pulled out the canteen, then walked over and handed it to her.

She quickly took it from him. "Thanks."

He watched as she opened the top and tipped the canteen up to her mouth. Some of the water missed her lips and drizzled down her chin. He was tempted to lap it up with his tongue. He had thought about tasting her that way a lot lately and intended to get his chance real soon.

He continued to watch her; getting turned on just from seeing how her throat moved as the cool liquid flowed down it. His eyes were so focused on her throat that he didn't notice that she had stopped drinking.

"Stone, you can have this back now."

He blinked. "Oh," he said, reaching for the canteen.

"Thanks again. The water was delicious."

"You're welcome. It's natural spring water," he said, thinking that she was delicious, too. Instead of putting the canteen away, he pulled the top back off and began drinking some of the water, deliberately tasting where her mouth had been.

When he finished he licked his lips, liking the hint of a taste of her that he had gotten from the canteen. He glanced up to see her watching him. She didn't say anything but just continued to look at him. And he looked at her. Then he felt it, that deep, hard throb in his gut that made him want to snatch her off the back of the horse and tumble with her in the grass. His body was already hot and was beginning to get hotter, in need of physical contact with her.

He saw how her cheeks darkened and he saw the moment desire filled her eyes. He also saw how fast the pulse was beating in her neck and the way she took out her tongue to moisten her already damp lips. His gaze slowly dropped to her blouse and saw how the nipples of her breasts were straining against the material. Her breathing, as well as his, was erratic. He heard it. He felt it. He wanted to taste it.

"You had enough?" he forced his gaze back to her eyes, as he tried like hell to get his thoughts and mind, and especially his body, back under control.

"Enough of what?" she asked, her voice soft, somewhat husky and definitely sensual. Her gaze was still holding his.

"Water."

She blinked and he saw that her features relayed both her confusion, as well as her longing for something she didn't quite understand yet. But she would in time. He would see to it. "Yes, I had enough," she said, after drawing in a deep breath.

He smiled. She hadn't had enough of anything yet. After putting her canteen back in her saddlebag he went around and got back on his horse. He leaned over and handed her reins to her. "Come on," he said huskily. "Let's continue our ride."

Six

Up until a half hour ago Madison thought she was hungry, but now something was affecting her appetite...or rather someone.

Stone Westmoreland.

She tilted her head as she watched him. He was standing some distance away tending to the horses. She was sitting on a stump eating one of the sandwiches Mrs. Quinn had packed for them and drinking a cold can of cola, while her eyes were glued to Stone.

She was attracted to him. There was no use denying it since that fact had already been established a few days ago. But what she couldn't understand was why she couldn't get past it. Why did a part of her want to act on it?

It seemed that although her mind was definitely on him, his mind was on the horses. He hadn't looked her way since they had stopped for lunch. She should have been grateful, but she couldn't deny being bothered by the fact that he could dismiss her so easily. But then, hadn't she laid out the ground rules last night? And hadn't those ground rules included a statement that anything developing between them was to be placed on the back burner? Evidently he had taken her at her word and intended to adhere to it.

She let out a deep sigh and the sound must have caught his attention. He lifted his eyes to hers, holding it for several long moments, saying nothing but looking at her. She met his gaze without flinching while desire stirred in her stomach, hot, thick, the likes of which she'd never experienced before. Without a sound, without a touch, and over the distance of twenty feet, she actually felt the heat of his gaze as tiny shocks of warmth began inching all the way up her spine to flow through her body. She even felt heat forming between her legs. Especially between her legs. And the appetite forming in her stomach had nothing to do with regular food. She continued to look at him while trying to cling to her composure, her resolve and her sanity.

Her throat tightened when he began walking toward her and the heat surging through her got hotter. She had never appreciated a Western shirt and tight jeans on a man until she had met him. She couldn't imagine his tall, muscled body wearing anything else…unless it was nothing at all.

Her breath caught. She wished she could strike that thought from her mind, call it back, and not think about it. But the deed was done. That wicked thought went right along with the dreams she'd been having about him lately. The man exuded raw sex appeal without trying and she was fully aware of him, more so than she needed to be.

"You okay?"

Madison shook her head. Not sure words would come out of her mouth even if she wanted them to, but she forced herself to speak anyway. "Yes, I'm fine, Stone."

He nodded as he continued to look at her. "Can I use some of that?" he asked indicating the small bottle of liquid hand sanitizer she had brought along.

"Sure, help yourself."

She watched as he uncapped the small bottle and poured some in his palm and then began rubbing his hands together in slow motion. She immediately thought of him rubbing those same hands all over her…in slow motion. She glanced at her soda can wondering if there was something inside it other than soda that was making her dizzy with such wanton thoughts.

"This is a beautiful spot, isn't it?"

His question got her attention. She shifted her gaze away from his hands to take in the beauty of their surroundings. "Yes, it is. I wish I had thought to bring a camera along."

He lifted a brow. "I'm surprised that you didn't."

She was surprised, too. "I had other things on my mind." And those *other things*, she told herself, were what she should be concentrating on and not on Stone. She continued to watch him as he recapped the hand sanitizer and placed it back in her gear. Then he walked over to his saddlebag to pull out his own sandwich and drink. She sighed. Maybe if she got him talking about his uncle she just might be able to clear her mind of hot, steamy thoughts. She figured it was worth a try.

"Do you have any idea who in Texas is trying to locate

your uncle, Stone?" she asked, after she had finished off the last of her sandwich.

He walked back over to her and sat down on the stump beside her. "No, I have no idea. I mentioned it to Durango and he didn't have a clue, either. We decided to turn it over to Quade and let him solve the mystery."

Madison lifted a brow. "Who?"

Stone smiled. "Quade. He's one of Durango's brothers—the one I mentioned was a twin. He used to be a secret service agent. Now he works for the government in some behind-the-scenes capacity. We don't have a clue exactly what he does. We see him when we see him and don't ask questions when we do. But we know how to contact him if we ever need him and usually within seventy-two hours we'll hear back from him."

Madison nodded. "And you think he can find out what's going on?"

"He'll find out."

Madison sat quietly for a moment thinking that Stone seemed pretty sure of his cousin's abilities. Her thoughts then shifted back to the man her mother had run off with. "Tell me about Corey Westmoreland," she said, feeling the need to know as much about him as she could since she would be coming face-to-face with him soon.

Stone glanced over at her after taking a sip of his soda. "Exactly what do you want to know?"

She shrugged. "What I'm really curious about is why everyone thinks it's strange for him to have a woman on his mountain."

Stone's lips lifted into a smile. "Mainly because as long as I can remember Uncle Corey claimed it would never happen. He's been involved with women before but none of them have ever been granted access to this mountain. He's always drawn the line as to how much of his life he's been willing to share with them."

Madison mulled this over for a second then said, "Yet he brought my mother here?"

"Yes, and that's what has me, Durango and the Quinns baffled."

Madison let out a deep sigh. "Now I'm beginning to wonder if perhaps they did know each other before."

Stone stared at her. "There is that possibility, but if I were you I wouldn't try to figure it out. Tomorrow you'll see them for yourself and can ask all the questions you want."

He reached across the distance and caught one of her hands in his and squeezed it gently. "But don't feel bad if she doesn't want to give you any answers. Maybe it's time for you to let your mother enjoy her life, Madison. After all, it's her life to live, isn't it?"

Although a frown appeared on Madison's face, she didn't say anything. Nor did she withdraw her hand from Stone's. All along he had given her food for thought and all along her mind had refused to accept what was becoming obvious.

"So when I see Corey Westmoreland, what should I expect?"

When he didn't answer right away, Madison assumed he was getting his thoughts together. "What you should expect is a fifty-four year old man who's been like a second father to his niece and eleven nephews. He's a man who believes in family, honor, respect and love for nature. For as long as I've known him, he has preferred solitude in some things and a vast amount of companionship in others. He won't hesitate to let you know how he feels on any subject and deeply respects the opinion of others."

A smile touched the corners of Stone's lips when he added, "And I learned early in life that he's also a man with eyes in the back of his head. You can't ever pull anything over on him."

The affection Madison heard in Stone's voice caused her to think just how different Corey Westmoreland was from her father. Her father had been an only child. He did have a cousin who'd also lived in Boston, but the two had never had a close relationship, so she hadn't developed a close relationship with thát cousin's children who were all around her age.

Her father had been born in the city, raised in the city and lived in the city. They'd never owned a pet while she was growing up and the thought of leaving the city to go camping wasn't anything he would have been interested in doing. And Larry Winters had preferred socializing to solitude, especially when it benefited him. He'd been a financial adviser. He would often host lavish parties for his clients with her mother acting as hostess. She remembered her father being excited each and every time they'd given a party, but now as she thought about it, her mother hadn't particularly cared for entertaining. She had merely accepted it as part of her role as the wife of a successful businessman. She tried to think of one single thing her parents had in common and couldn't think of anything. Last night Stone had asked her why two people who possibly didn't love each other would stay together. Now her question was why had they gotten married in the first place?

She came out of her reverie when Stone removed his hand from hers. She sat quietly and watched him finish off the rest of his sandwich and down the last of his soda. He then glanced over at her and studied her as if she was going to be his dessert. Visibly feeling the heat of his gaze and not able to sit and take it any longer, she stood and glanced around.

Stone studied Madison for a long moment then asked, "How are you holding up so far?"

She shrugged. "I'm fine. Usually I have an over-abundance of energy. It takes a lot to wear me out."

Stone's gaze drifted down the length of her body. He would definitely remember that later. He watched as she picked up her hat and placed it back on her head.

"Don't you think we should move on if we plan to make it to that cabin before nightfall?" she asked.

He stood and flashed her a slow, sexy grin. "Yeah, Miss Winters, I think that you're right."

The cabin was not what either Stone or Madison had expected. What they assumed they would find was a small one-room structure. But what Martin Quinn and McKinnon had built in the clearing—nestled between large pine trees with a breathtaking view of the mountains and valleys for a backdrop, as well as a beautiful stream running at the back of it—was a cabin large enough to be used as a home away from home.

Stone and Madison took a quick tour of the place. The outside of the cabin featured an inviting wraparound porch. Inside, there was a huge living room with a fireplace, two bedrooms connected by a large single bathroom, and an eat-in kitchen with an enormous window that overlooked the stream out back. It didn't take long for Stone to discover that they would have electricity once he fired up the generator and the linen closets had fresh sheets and coverings for the bed.

Stone sighed, grateful that they had made it to the cabin before nightfall. They still had a few hours of daylight left and he would use the time to feed and care for the horses and start the generator.

He glanced over at Madison who was silently standing beside him. Like him her gaze was on the two bedrooms and he could swear he'd heard her deep sigh of relief.

"I've got a few things to do outside," he said, breaking the silence between them.

She nodded. "Okay and I can work to get the fireplace going. I have a feeling it's going to be rather cold tonight."

Stone met her gaze, deciding not to tell her that he would be more than happy to provide her with all the heat she would need. "All right, I'll be back later."

It was a full hour or so before Stone returned. Madison had taken advantage of his absence to take a shower. He inhaled the soft, seductive and arousing scent of her the moment he walked into the cabin and came to a dead stop when she walked out of the bedroom.

She had changed into a pair of sweatpants with a tank top; something she must have found more comfortable than jeans. No matter what the woman put on her body, it looked elegant as hell on her. Madison Winters was definitely one class act. Her hair was no longer pulled back in a ponytail but its silky, luxurious strands flowed in sexy disarray about her shoulders. He growled deep in his throat, resisting the urge to cross the room and pull her into his arms and get a real good taste of her; something he'd been dying to do all day.

She glanced up and saw him staring at her. She stared back at him for a moment without saying anything, then a nervous smile touched the corners of her lips. "Although I was tempted, I didn't use up all the hot water. There's plenty left if you want to go ahead and take your bath."

"That sounds rather nice," he said, his voice sounding hoarse. He wanted to take a bath and soak his tired, aching muscles but something had him rooted in place and he couldn't seem to move from that spot.

He continued to stare at her while his insides ached, throbbed. A long period of silence suspended every sound, except for his breathing…and hers. They both jumped when a piece of burning log crackled in the fireplace. Stone shifted his gaze from hers to the fire. "It feels real good in here. Thanks for getting the fire started," he said, although his mind was on another type of fire altogether.

She shrugged. "It was the least I could do while you were outside taking care of the horses and getting the generator started. And I took the liberty to unpack dinner. Mrs. Quinn sent a container of beef stew for us to eat. It's warming now."

Stone nodded and sniffed the air. There was the faint smell of the stew. He hadn't picked up on it when he'd come inside. The only scent his nostrils had caught had been of her. "Smells good."

"It should be ready by the time you have finished your bath."

He nodded. "All right. I guess I'd better get to it then."

Seconds passed and he still didn't move. He continued to look at her. Absorb everything about her.

"Stone?"

He blinked. "Yes?"

"Your bath."

A slow smile touched his lips. "Oh, yeah. I'll be back in a minute." He crossed the floor into the other bedroom and closed the door.

As soon as Stone pulled the door shut behind him, he leaned against it and hooked his fingers into the belt loops of his jeans as he tried to get his body under control. He felt blood surge through his body, making him swell in one particular area. He needed to get out of his jeans real quick-like or the force of his arousal that was straining against his zipper would kill him or at least injure him for life.

Part of his plan had been to lay temptation at Madison's feet but she was unknowingly laying it at his. He'd thought with all the chores he'd had to do outside that he would have worked off some of his nervous energy. But as soon as he'd seen her, the only thing he'd managed to do was to work up an oversize case of sexual need.

A prickle of unease made its way up his spine. For Madison to be someone who knew nothing about passion, she definitely looked like a woman who could deliver. And he had a feeling that that delivery would be so much to his liking that he might start getting crazy ideas about wanting to keep her around.

He closed his eyes and clenched his jaw tight. The last thing he needed was to think of any woman in permanent terms. And he refused to let a beautiful, proper-talking, brown-eyed, delectable-smelling city woman come into his life and change things. All he needed to do was remember that episode with Durango a few years ago to screw his head back on tight. The first time his womanizing cousin had let his guard down and fallen for a city woman, he'd been left with scars for life.

But then Stone knew Madison was nothing like the woman who had ripped out Durango's heart. Madison Winters wasn't like any woman he knew. He'd been so hell-bent on introducing her to sexual pleasures that he'd outright forgotten how long it had been for him. He hadn't slept with a woman in over a year after practically shutting off his social life to complete his last book. And the last few women he had been involved with had been downright bores. The need for physical intimacy was tugging at his insides, making him feel things he normally didn't feel; making him want something he usually didn't think twice about doing without.

But still, when all was said and done, no matter what torture he was going through, the woman in the other room was his main concern. Her needs outweighed his and more than anything she needed to understand how it felt to be driven to lose control, to act impulsively and to be spontaneous. She deserved to experience reckless pleasure and uncontrollable passion at least once. And as he moved away from the door and walked toward the connecting bathroom, he knew he wanted that one time to be with him.

Madison placed her hand on her forehead, feeling her skin and wondering why she was beginning to feel so hot. But deep down she knew the reason why. Anytime she was within close proximity to Stone, her temperature went up a few degrees. There was no way she could deny that she wanted him. And hearing the sound of the bath running and knowing that he was in the bathroom naked and wet wasn't helping matters.

Ninety-six hours was the equivalent of four days. That's how long she had known him and here she was thinking all kinds of naughty thoughts. There were still some things about Storm Westmoreland that she didn't know, but she felt certain there was a fair amount that she did know. She had a feeling that the same description he had given his uncle earlier that day could also be used to describe him.

During the ride up the mountain he talked about his family and she knew he was close to them and that all the Westmorelands had a special relationship. And she knew that he also had a love and deep appreciation for nature. That was evident when he had pointed out various plants and trees, as well as telling her about the different types of wildlife that was found in these parts. And she had a feeling there were times in his life—possibly while working on one of his novels—that he sought solitude more often than others. But at the same time he would feel comfortable in any type of social gathering if that was where he wanted to belong.

And she knew that although he would be the last person to brag about his work, she'd heard her girlfriends say countless times that he was an excellent storyteller. She even remembered one of her friends staying overnight at her place after reading one of his thriller-chiller novels, because she was frightened. That was one of the reasons Madison had decided never to read his books. She lived alone in her apartment and the last thing she needed was to start looking over her shoulder or waking up during the night at the slightest sound.

Madison had discovered after reading the newspaper at breakfast yesterday morning that Stone's latest book, *Whispers of a Stalker,* was still on the *New York Times* bestseller list even after twelve weeks. During the ride today, Stone had also shared with her information about his involvement on a national level with the Teach the People to Read program—a program aimed at fighting illiteracy.

Another thing she believed with all her heart was that he was someone who could be trusted. She had felt comfortable with him from the first and the thought of them alone in this cabin, miles from civilization, didn't bother her.

Yes, she decided to admit, it *did* bother her, especially when it stirred something inside her each and every time he looked at her with promises of untold pleasures in his eyes. Pleasures she'd never had before.

She walked to the window and looked out. It was dark and everything around them appeared black and still. She had actually seen a bald eagle fly overhead, but she might have missed the experience if Stone hadn't pointed it out to her.

"What are you thinking about, Madison?"

Madison quickly spun around, holding shaking fingers to her chest. She hadn't heard Stone approach. In fact she had been listening to the sound of the water running during his bath and wondered at what point he'd turned it off.

He was standing in the middle of the kitchen wearing another pair of jeans and a T-shirt with the words, The Rolling Stone, boldly displayed across his large, muscular chest. His hair was damp and she felt like crossing the distance separating them and rubbing her hand over his head. And that wasn't the only thing she wanted to rub her hands over, she thought as he held her gaze. His eyes blazed with a deep heat. She may not be experienced in some things, but she could definitely recognize sexual desire in a man; especially this man. It had been in his gaze the first time his eyes had met hers.

"So, you want to keep whatever it was you were thinking a secret?" he asked with a rueful smile.

Madison sighed, turned back to the window. "I was just thinking how quiet things seem outside and yet I know there are plenty of animals out there that make this area their home. In a way I feel as if we are invading their territory."

She felt the heat of him when he came to stand beside her. "Invasion is fine as long as we don't do anything to destroy their natural environment."

She nodded and turned and almost collided with him. She hadn't been aware that he had been standing so close.

"There's something else I've discovered about invasions," he said, holding her gaze.

Madison knew her control was about to be tested. "What?"

"It can make some people rather uncomfortable. Like right now. I am invading your space, aren't I?"

Madison nodded. Yes, he was invading her space but she didn't feel uncomfortable or threatened by it. Instead she felt an incredible magnetism, an intrinsic sensual pull to him.

"Madison?"

She inhaled, pulling air into her lungs before answering, "Yes, but I don't mind sharing my space with you, Stone. Are you ready for dinner?"

She watched as a smile curved his sensuous lips. "I'm ready for a lot a things."

She didn't want to read between the lines but did so anyway. Visions of just what those other things might be danced around in her head. She tried holding on to the decisions she had made yesterday morning about their relationship and discovered she was having a hard time doing so. She cleared her throat. "I'll put the food on the table."

Without giving him a chance to say anything else, she walked off toward the kitchen cabinets to take down a couple of bowls.

"The stew's good, isn't it?"

The sound of Stone's husky voice drifted across the table and was as intimate as a caress. Madison glanced up from eating her stew and met his gaze. A part of her shivered inside from the visual contact. More than once she had caught him staring at her, and against her will her body had responded, each and every time.

Common sense demanded that she fight her interest in him, but it was hard to dredge up will power or common sense around a man like Stone. "Yes, it's delicious," she said trying not to feel the warmth that was spreading through her belly.

Stone pushed his bowl aside, licking his lips. "Too bad we don't have anything for dessert."

Madison swallowed, eyeing his lips with interest. Oh, she could think of a few things she had definitely developed a sweet tooth for over the last few days. His kisses topped the list. "Yes, it is, isn't it?" she decided it was safer to say.

"I'll help you with dishes," Stone said, getting to his feet.

Madison considered his offer and quickly decided that it wouldn't be a good idea. Earlier she'd told him that she didn't mind him in her space but at the moment she needed him out of it to get her mind focused. "There's no need. I only have a few items to take care of anyway."

"You sure?" he asked.

"Yes, I'm positive. I'd think you'd want to retire early. Today has to have been an exhausting one for you."

Stone's throaty chuckle swirled over her like a sensual mist, absorbing her, snarling her and making desire ripple through her. "No, usually I have an overabundance of energy. It takes a lot to wear me out."

She recognized his words as similar to ones she'd spoken earlier that day. She came to her feet and gathered their dishes off the table. Deep down she was aware of the electrical tension that was beginning to short circuit in her body, however she was determined not to go up in smoke.

She walked over to the kitchen sink, feeling the heat of Stone's stare; she tried hard to ignore it. His very presence and the scent of him taunted her with the unknown and, although her back was to him, she was aware of every move he made and every breath he took.

Her pulse rate increased when she heard him get up from the table and cross the room to stand less than two feet behind her, and for a few moments he stood silently, not saying anything, not doing anything. Then he took another step, reducing the distance separating them and she quickly turned around.

Their gazes collided. His was so intense the force of it ripped through her, sending a sharp sexual longing to her belly, between her legs and to her breasts; making her nipples harden in immediate response.

Then she felt herself moving, taking a step forward and reaching out to drape her arms around his neck. She heard the growl he made, deep in his throat, just moments, mere seconds, before he claimed her mouth with a kiss that seduced any resistance she may have had out of her.

The heated, yet gentle thrust of his tongue as it slipped between her lips had her whimpering in pleasure, and he toyed and teased with her tongue while sharing his taste and the intensity of his hunger. She was trying hard to understand what was happening to her. Then she decided, why bother. Who could possibly understand how Stone was making her feel? Who could understand why her heart was beating five times its normal rate and how the heat of him was branding her all over, especially in the area between her legs to the point that she felt her panties getting wet. And when he pressed his body up against her, bringing her closer and letting her feel the magnitude and strength of his arousal, she emitted a soft moan. He was stroking a flame within her and she was a willing victim. She didn't want to dwell on the decisions she had made yesterday morning. The only thing she wanted to think about was how he was making her feel.

She felt him pulling his mouth away and thought, *no, not yet* and tightened her arms around him, keeping their mouths locked, as her tongue became the aggressor, doing what his had done to her earlier. She licked the insides of his mouth from point A to point Z, exploring, tasting, consuming as much of him as she could, but still feeling it wasn't enough. Her body had broken free of any restraints and was raging with an intense sexual need that only he could fill.

He broke free from their kiss and she whimpered in protest until she felt him lift her top and his mouth latch on to one of her nipples. She had forgotten she hadn't worn a bra and the touch of his tongue to her breast, sucking, flicking and licking like he was getting the dessert he talked about earlier. She moaned deep in her throat as coils of sexual need tightened deep within her.

He pulled back slightly and she felt herself being lifted effortlessly into his arms. "I want you," he whispered, his voice hot next to her ear.

She wanted him, too, and reached out and pulled his mouth back down to hers. Tonight they were in a cabin deep in the wilderness and succumbing to the call of the wild. She felt out of control with him and knew whatever he wanted to do she wanted to do, too. Never in her life had she wanted or needed a man with this much intensity. She hadn't known such a thing was possible.

He lifted his mouth from hers and she felt herself being carried swiftly out of the kitchen and straight into one of the bedrooms; the one he had planned to use. He placed her on the bed and immediately went to her clothes, pulling the top over her head and easing her sweatpants down her legs.

Heat soared through her as he removed her panties and she knew he was aware just how wet they were. But he didn't say anything, merely tossed them aside. His gaze was still on her, penetrating and compelling. Then he reached out and skimmed his hand across her femininity, as if using his fingers to test her readiness and the degree of her need. She groaned, threw her head back and opened her legs to give him access and he took it.

"Damn, you're hot and wet," he murmured hoarsely against her ear as his tongue moved over her face to lick the perspiration off her throat and he worked his way up to her chin. He inched his way farther upward and his tongue parted her lips, seeking her taste once again.

But after a moment, that wasn't enough for him. His mouth began moving lower like he was obsessively hungry for her. His tongue worked its way past her breasts and down her chest to her navel, torturing every inch of her in the process. Then he reached the very essence of her heat and used his mouth and tongue to drive her mad in a very intimate French kiss.

She screamed as her body shook with a force that had her digging her fingers into his shoulders to stop the room from spinning, the earth from shaking and her body from splintering in two. The feel of his mouth on her touched off an explosion but still he wouldn't let up. It was as if he was determined to have it all and, in the process, give her everything. Her body was thrown into an orgasm of gigantic proportions that had her nearly sobbing in pleasure and before she could recover from that first orgasm, his mouth and tongue was busy sending her whirling into a second as he once again pushed her over the edge.

Moments later, while she lay there trying to learn how to breathe all over again, he stood back away from the bed and began removing his shirt. She barely had enough strength to prop her elbows on the bed to watch him, studying how well defined his chest was and how a thin line of dark hair led a path downward, past the waistband of his jeans.

She continued to watch, fascinated, and knew at that moment she had never seen a more perfectly made male body. She could stare all day and not tire of seeing it. She held her breath as he slowly eased down his zipper. Then he pulled off his jeans and briefs, letting her see all of him. Her gaze immediately went to his shaft, thick, large and hard, protruding like a statue from the bed of dark curls that surrounded it. She almost swallowed her tongue.

"I want you," he said huskily, coming back to join her on the bed after putting on the condom he had taken from the pocket of his jeans. "Come here, baby, and let me show you how much."

She eagerly went into his arms and felt her body shudder when her bare skin made contact with his. He took her into his arms and kissed her again. It was as if she hadn't had two orgasms already. Her body was getting aroused all over again. The ache began throbbing between her legs and she knew it would take more than his mouth and tongue this time to satisfy what ailed her there.

He evidently knew it, too. She heard his low groan as he eased her back against the pillows. "I want it all. I want to give you something you've never had before," he whispered huskily in her ear.

She opened her mouth to tell him that he'd already given her something she hadn't ever had before, twice. But he kissed her, silencing her words, drugging her senses and stirring up a need within her that demanded more. Their gazes held, locked and she became ensnarled by the heat in his eyes.

Stone inhaled deeply as he struggled to maintain control. He couldn't last much longer without getting inside of her, needing to be there as much as he needed his next breath. He had tasted her and now he wanted to mate with her, become a part of her, thrust deep and stay forever if there was any way that he could. He moved his body over hers, not breaking eye contact.

"Let me ease inside," he whispered huskily, and she shifted her body to accommodate his request. Then he leaned forward, captured her mouth and kissed her again, wanting to convey without words just how he felt. He rotated the lower part of his body, letting his shaft caress her, seek her out and he found her wet, slick and hot.

He lifted his mouth as his hands gripped her hips. When she began closing her eyes he knew he wanted her to look at him, he wanted to see the expression on her face the moment their bodies joined. "Open your eyes. Look at me, Madison. I want to see you when you take me in."

Her gaze held his and her fingers began stroking his shoulders as she parted her legs for him. Not able, nor willing to hold back any longer Stone eased inside of her. He sucked in a deep breath and his hands held her hips in a firm grip as he continued going as deep as he could, feeling the muscles of her body clench him, take him, claim him.

And then he established a rhythm, slow and easy; the fast and hard thrusting in and out in an urgency that enveloped them. He groaned deep in his throat as he gave her all of him and took all of her in the process. He felt the tremors that began radiating through her body when he increased his rhythmic pace, stroking her, as well as himself into an explosion. He threw his head back and felt the muscles in his neck strain, and when she screamed his name, he lifted her hips to lock her legs around him to share in the orgasm that was overtaking her.

He growled out her name between clenched teeth and when the shudders began wracking her body, he felt it; something he had never felt before. Passion yes. Satiated hunger—that, too. But there was something else he felt and when he buried his face against her neck, he pushed out of his mind whatever it was. The only thing he wanted at that moment was to share in the aftereffects of such a beautiful mating.

He shifted his weight off her and pulled her into his arms. He somehow found the strength to lean up and look at her. A smile, a deep, satisfied smile, drifted across her lips and the gaze holding his was filled with joy and wonder. Utter satisfaction. And he knew they had shared something special and unique. They had shared passion of the most unbridled and the richest kind, and he knew that before they left this cabin they would do so again, and again and again....

Seven

Stone lay propped up on his elbow as he gazed down at the sleeping woman beside him in the bed. What Madison had said yesterday had been true. She possessed an over-abundance of energy and it took a lot to wear her out.

He couldn't help but smile when he thought of the number of times they had made love during the night; her body taking him in, clenching him, satisfying him and demanding from him all that he could give. And he had given a lot; all he had and they had made love until exhaustion had wracked their bodies. It was only then that she had fallen asleep in his arms, her limbs entwined with his. He'd managed to get some sleep in, as well, but now he was wide-awake and fully aroused. He wanted her again. He glanced down at their bodies, seemingly joined at the hips and liked what he saw. He liked it too much.

Taking a deep breath, full realization hit him and he accepted that he had shared something with Madison that he had never shared with any other woman. A lot of himself. No, he had shared *all* of himself. For her he had let his guard down.

His gaze dropped back down to her and latched on to her bare breasts. This attraction he had for her was nothing but lust, he tried convincing himself, but then he remembered how he felt emotionally, each and every time she had screamed out his name while swept up in the throes of ecstasy. Okay, he admitted he would always remember last night, but he refused to get hung up on it and start reading more into it than was there. He had wanted to introduce her to passion, and he had. No big deal. He had wanted to show her how two levelheaded individuals could suddenly become overtaken with desire, a desire so consuming that it could stir uncontrollable passion between them. And he'd done that, too. The only thing left was for them to find her mother and Uncle Corey.

He frowned when he thought what would probably happen after that. Once Madison saw her mother and was reassured that she was fine, she'd probably return to Boston. He, on the other hand, would go back to Durango's place and do what he'd intended to do from the beginning. He would get a little R and R before starting work on his next book.

Why did the thought of them going their separate ways begin to gnaw on his insides? Why did the thought of her sharing her newfound passion with another man bother the hell out of him? He had made love to other women and never felt troubled by the thought of them sleeping with someone else after their relationship ended. In fact, he'd always been grateful that his ex-lovers wanted to move on.

He inhaled deeply. He needed distance from Madison to think straight and to get his head back on right. She was making him feel things no other woman had made him feel and he didn't like it worth a damn.

Easing from her side, he slipped out of bed and quickly pulled on his jeans, not bothering to put on his briefs or a shirt. He didn't want her to wake up for fear that he wouldn't know how he would handle things.

Before walking out of the bedroom he glanced back and wished that he hadn't. His gaze roamed over her. She was curled on her side with a satiated smile on her lips while she slept. She looked like a woman made for passion and every muscle in his body ached to make love to her again.

He forced his gaze away as a thickness settled in his throat at the same time as one formed in his midsection. Stone slowly shook his head. He needed distance and he needed it now. Quickly walking out of the room, he closed the door behind him.

Madison stirred awake and squinted her eyes against the bright sunlight that was coming in through the window. She stretched and immediately felt the soreness in muscles she hadn't used in a long time. She smiled. She had definitely used them last night.

Pulling herself up in bed she glanced around, wondering where Stone had gone. She knew they had planned to get an early start to reach his uncle's place before nightfall but now she felt downright lazy. She didn't want to do anything but stay in bed and wait for his return.

She drew in a shuddering breath when she remembered all the things they had done the night before. He had introduced her to passion of the most sensual kind. She had felt emotions and had done things with Stone that she had never felt or done with her former fiancé. A blushing heat stole into her features when she thought how Stone had touched her all over, tasted her all over, made love to her all over. Even now his scent was drenched into her skin. Her nostrils were filled with the aroma of him: manly, robust and sexy.

What was there about Stone Westmoreland that had made her throw caution to the wind and do what she'd done? What was there about him that made her eager to do it again?

When moments passed and Stone didn't return to bed, and she didn't hear any movement or sound from the opposite side of the bedroom door, she wondered where he had gone and decided to find out. What was he thinking this morning? Did he regret what they'd done? Did he think she assumed that now that they'd made love she expected something from him? She remembered distinctly him saying that he wasn't the marrying kind. He believed strongly in the institution but also believed that marriage wasn't for him. He had no plans ever to settle down. He had told her that he liked his life just the way it was. He enjoyed the freedom of coming and going whenever he pleased and not being responsible for anyone but himself. He didn't want any worries, no bothers and definitely no wife.

She sighed deeply as she slipped out of bed. She glanced around for the clothes she had discarded the night before and decided that, instead of putting them back on, she would slip into Stone's shirt. It hit her midthigh and she liked the way it looked on her because it symbolized that she was his and he was hers.

She shook her head, wondering where that thought had come from and decided not to think that way again. Stone wasn't looking for a serious relationship and neither was she. Opening the door she knew she had to pull herself together before seeing him. The last thing she needed was to put more into her relationship with him than was really there.

Madison searched the house and found no sign of Stone. She stepped outside onto the porch. Then she saw him. He was in the distance, shirtless and riding without a saddle. Instead, a blanket covered the animal's back.

She leaned against the column post and watched him. He had told her that he knew how to handle a horse and she'd seen firsthand how well he did so on their trek up the mountains. He had explained that his uncle had made sure his eleven nephews and one niece learned how to ride and had taken the time to teach each one of them how to handle a horse when they came to visit. She had to admit that those lessons had paid off. It was evident that Stone was a skilled horseman. He even shared with her that he owned a horse that was stabled at Highpoint Manor, a place where he could go and enjoy the Georgia Mountains on horseback. From Atlanta it would take him less than two hours to reach the Blue Ridge Mountains where he would get on the back of his horse for an excursion into the wilderness.

Something made him look her way and her breath caught when he saw her. He trotted the horse over to her, coming to a stop by the porch. "Good morning, Madison."

"Good morning, Stone."

Some part of her felt she should be embarrassed after how she'd acted last night and everything they had done together. But she felt no shame. In fact she wasn't even feeling self-conscious that she was standing before him wearing his shirt without a stitch of clothing underneath. It seemed that all her proper Boston upbringing had gone back up North without her, leaving her doing and thinking all sorts of naughty things.

She tipped her head back to look at him. He was sitting on the horse looking sexier than any man had a right to look. Their gazes locked, held and she felt a quickening in her stomach. She also felt a stirring heat between her legs and as he continued to gaze down at her, she saw the color of his eyes darken as desire flooded their depths.

"Come ride with me," he said throatily. His voice was so husky it sent a sensuous chill down her spine.

Without asking where they were going or bothering to bring to his attention the fact that she wasn't appropriately dressed to go riding, she accepted the hand he reached out to her. He leaned over and, with one smooth sweep, gathered her into his arms. However, instead of placing her on the horse behind him, he placed her in front of him turning her to face him. When she lifted a brow in surprise, he said, "You're beautiful and I can't help but want to look at you this morning."

Madison smiled, touched by his comment. "But how will you see to lead the horse with me blocking your view?"

A grin touched the corners of his mouth. "You won't be blocking it. Besides, I get the feeling this horse has been up here several times and knows his way around. I pretty much let him lead the way."

Madison nodded, then held on as Stone urged the horse into a trot. When they got a little distance from the cabin he slowed the horse down to a walking pace. At first she had felt uncomfortable facing him while sitting on the back of a horse, especially with the way he was looking at her, but another feeling was taking over. It didn't help matters when the horse came to a complete stop and began nibbling on the grass. Stone decided to use that time to nibble on her. He leaned forward and captured her lips, kissing her with an intensity that set her body on fire. She encircled his neck with her arms for support while enjoying their kiss.

"Aren't you afraid that we're going to fall off this horse?" she asked him when he pulled his mouth away moments later.

"No. It's just like anything else you ride," he responded, his tone breathy and hot. "You have to keep your balance."

She wondered how a person could keep their balance when their mind was spinning. Stone's kiss had rocked her world and she was dizzy from the impact. He had stroked her tongue with his, causing the heat that was already settled inside of her to go up another degree.

"You look good in my shirt," he said, before reaching out and undoing the top button. Then the second and third.

"Stone, what are you doing?" she asked in a startled gasp, barely getting the words out when he had eased buttons four and five free. She brought her hands up to cover his.

"Undressing you."

Madison could clearly see that. She glanced around. "But, but, we're outside in the open."

"Yes, but we're also alone. No one is here but you, me and this horse, and he's too busy filling his stomach to worry about what we're doing."

"Yes, but—"

That was as far as she got when Stone recaptured her mouth and at the same moment gently slid off the horse with her in his arms, snagging the blanket in the process.

When he ended the kiss and placed her on her feet, she met his gaze and he thought about how different she was from all the other women he had been with. With Madison, he had no control and he wondered if she knew just how seductive she was. He had a feeling that she didn't have a clue.

Stone had left her alone in the cabin because he'd needed distance to think, but all he'd done while out riding was think about her. He couldn't erase from his mind how she had made him feel when she had run her hands over him, sending shock waves of pleasure through his body. Nor could he forget how she had smiled at him after they had both reached their pleasure, snuggling closer to him, resting her head against his chest and going to sleep in his arms like it was just where she wanted to be. Just where she belonged.

With that memory firmly imbedded in his mind, he reached up and began stroking her hair, needing to touch her, to feel connected. He watched with penetrating attentiveness as her breathing quickened, her eyes darkened and her lips parted.

He gently cupped the back of her neck and drew her closer to his face. Bringing her lips just inches from his, he whispered, "I want to make love to you, here, under the Montana sky."

He watched as her eyes drifted closed and when she reopened them, the eyes that looked at him were filled with desire, as well as uncertainty. He wanted to keep the for-

mer and remove the latter. He reached for her hand and
began slowly stroking her wrist in a slow seductive motion
and watched as the uncertainty in her gaze faded.

"I want to make love to you under the Montana sky,
too," she whispered when only desire shone in the depths
of her dark eyes. Her voice was so low he could barely hear
the words.

Stone drew in a sharp intake of breath as the intensity
of just how much he wanted Madison hit him. Taking her
hand in his, he led her through a path that was shrouded
with lush green prairie grass. When he found what he
thought was the perfect spot, he spread the blanket on the
ground, sat down and pulled her on to his lap.

His mouth captured hers and with a shaking hand, he
removed his shirt from her body. Moments later, he pulled
back and stood to remove his jeans; taking a condom pack
from the pocket before tossing them aside. His hand continued to shake as he sheathed himself.

He is a beautiful man, Madison thought as she watched
what Stone was doing. A sheen of perspiration covered his
chest; a chest she knew was broad and muscular. Then there
were those strong thighs, firm buttocks and the huge erec-
tion that promised more of what they'd shared last night.

She inhaled deeply. A slow throbbing ache had started
low and deep in her stomach, inching its way through every
part of her body. She actually felt a climax building and
Stone hadn't done anything but kiss her…but the look in
his eyes promised everything. And she wanted it all.

She wanted Stone Westmoreland.

She didn't want to think about the implications of what
that might mean. At the moment she couldn't give herself

that luxury. The only thoughts she wanted flowing through her mind were intimate ones. She forced the lump in her throat away, as a little voice in the back of her mind whispered, *live for the moment. Enjoy this time with him to the fullest.*

After Stone finished putting on the condom he paused as his gaze held Madison's. Last night while making love, he had never felt so connected, so joined, so linked to a woman. It was as if they had formed a kinship, an unshakable attachment, a special bond that he couldn't dismiss even if he wanted to.

Maybe it was pure insanity on his part to think that way. In that case, he might as well call himself crazy because the thoughts were in his head and there wasn't a damn thing he could do about them now. He would have to figure things out later because what he wanted more than anything, even more than his next breath, was the woman who was sitting on the blanket watching every move he made with so much desire in her eyes, it only made his body harder.

He let out a deep breath and wondered how he could have gone through life for thirty-three years and not known of her existence. She was beautiful, exquisite and, for now, right this minute, she was his.

His.

He swallowed deeply, knowing he had to say something and that he needed to choose his words carefully. He wanted her to know, he *had* to let her know, that this wasn't just another coupling for him. What they shared all through last night, as well as what they were about to share now were special to him and totally out of sync with how he usually did things. He wanted her to know she had touched him in a way that no woman had done before.

When he moved his mouth to say the words, Madison leaned forward, reached out and placed her fingers to his lips. She wasn't ready to hear what he had to say, especially if it was something that would break the romantic spell between them. She didn't want to hear him stress once again the kind of man that he was. She knew that he was not looking for a serious involvement and she respected that, but neither of them could turn their backs on the passion that was now raging between them. Right now, all she wanted to think about—all she cared about—was that this wonderful man had given her a real taste of passion, something she had never experienced before. He'd also shown her how it felt to fall for someone.

And she had fallen helplessly and hopelessly in love with Stone Westmoreland.

He pulled her fingers from his lips and leaned forward, brushing those same lips against hers before letting the fullness of his mouth settle over hers, kissing her with an intensity that sent heat soaring through her veins. The same wanting, longing and desire that she had encountered from the moment she'd met him took over and she pulled him down to her, determined to make this morning a repeat of last night.

He broke off the kiss and his hands and mouth went to work to drive her insanely out of her mind. She twisted and moaned beneath him sighing his name and reaching out to capture in her hands that part of him she wanted so badly.

When she held his thick arousal in her hand she folded her fingers around him, squeezing him in her palm. She looked up, met his gaze and asked, "Ready?"

The heat from his gaze nearly scorched her insides and when he smiled she became entrenched in passion so intense she could barely breathe. "Ready," he replied.

She let go and the solid length of him probed her feminine folds as he rolled his hips, finding the rhythm he intended for them to share. Sweat appeared on his forehead and she knew he was just as over the edge as she was, just as hungry for this.

Lowering his head, he captured her mouth, sought out her tongue at the same exact moment that he entered her, swallowing the moan that came from deep in her throat. He lifted her hips and wrapped her legs around him as he went deeper. She felt all of him, every single inch of his intimate flesh. He thrust back and forth inside her as he deepened the kiss they were sharing.

Stone released her mouth when a growl erupted deep in his throat. Sensations spiraled through him. He increased their rhythm and his body began moving faster, his thrusts became harder and went deeper. All of him worked tirelessly to satisfy this woman he was making love with and when he felt her body begin shuddering in an orgasm that made her cry out, he knew he had again succeeded.

He threw his head back as his thrusts quickened even more and he knew that, for as long as he lived, he would have memories of the time he had made love to her under a Montana sky. When he felt her body explode in another climax, he was there with her and continued to pump into her until he had nothing left to give.

"Stone!"

"Madison!"

Everything transformed into one sensuously dizzy moment and he captured her mouth, needing to be joined with her from the top all the way to the bottom. And she returned his kiss the same way he was giving it to her, responding to every delicious stroke of his tongue.

Moments later, Stone slid from her body and gathered her into his arms to hold her as she slumped against him. She tucked her face into the warmth of his neck, and he couldn't help but wonder just how he would handle things when she returned to Boston.

"Are you sure that you won't mind staying here another night?"

Madison looked across the kitchen table at Stone. They had made love once again after returning to the cabin and drifted off to sleep. Hunger had awakened them a few hours later and after dressing—or half-dressing, since she had put his shirt back on and he was wearing only his jeans—they had stumbled into the kitchen. For two people who prided themselves on possessing endless energy, they were definitely wearing each other out.

Surprisingly, the kitchen cupboards weren't bare. There were a number of cans of soup and they decided to share some tomato soup.

"Yes, I'm sure, as long as we have something to eat." She smiled. "Besides, it would be dangerous to travel if we were to leave now. Soon it will be dark."

Stone nodded then reached across the table and captured her hand in his. "Do you regret that we didn't head out first thing this morning as we'd planned?"

She met his gaze. "No."

They went back to bed and made love again and later,

after dressing fully, they decided to take a walk around the cabin. "Have you prepared yourself for tomorrow?" Stone asked, holding her hand as they walked along the stream.

Madison glanced up at him. A beautiful sunset was emerging before them and she had a beautiful man to share it with.

"No, I've been so caught up in what we've been doing that I haven't had a chance to really think about it. And maybe that's a good thing."

"Why?"

"Because sharing this time with you has opened my eyes to a lot of things. I hate to think of my parents' love life, but what if my mother never experienced anything as rich and profound as the passion we've shared in the whole time she was married to my father?"

Stone hugged her tighter to him. "Maybe your parents were passionately in love at one point." But he knew what she meant. He also knew that his uncle had a way with women and he couldn't help but wonder if perhaps, when he saw Abby Winters, he had detected untapped passion in her in the same way Stone had detected it in Madison.

"But I plan to do as you suggested, Stone."

Her words intruded on his thoughts and he glanced down at her. "What is that?"

"Keep an open mind about things and not be judgmental."

He nodded. "I'm sure your mother would appreciate that. She'll probably be surprised as hell to see you. The last thing she needs is for you to become the parent and make her feel like a naughty child."

Madison sighed deeply. "Do you think I made a mistake by even coming?"

He put his hand on her wrist to stop them from walking any farther, knowing he had to be honest with her. "At first I did, but now I know it's just your nature. You were concerned about her. I think she will understand that."

Madison hoped so. The closer the time came to seeing her mother, the more she began to feel nervous about her motives in pursuing her. What right did she have to interfere in her mother's life? Her mother was a fifty-year-old woman and if she was going through a midlife crisis then it was her business. She shook her head. Her mother was the only family she had so anything her mother was going through was both of their businesses. She would just have to adjust her way of thinking about things and practice understanding. And thanks to the man standing in front of her, she believed that she could. Stone had shown her the true meaning of passion and the pleasures of making love. And he had also introduced her to the joys of loving and Madison now knew that she truly loved him.

Once things were settled with her mother, she would leave immediately for Boston. The memories she would have of the time she and Stone had spent together would keep her warm on those lonely nights when she would long to have him naked in bed beside her; those times when she would yearn for her dreams of him to become reality. Already the thought of leaving him caused pain to pierce her heart, but she would survive…she had no other choice.

Eight

Wow! That was the one word that immediately came to Madison's mind when they reached the top of the mountain where Corey Westmoreland lived.

Coming to Montana had certainly opened her eyes to the beauty of an area she had never visited before. Seeing the spacious and sprawling ranch house in the distance, set among a stand of pine trees and beneath the beautiful Montana blue sky, forced a breathless sigh to escape from her lips.

"Why would one man need a place so huge?" she turned and asked Stone.

His mouth twitched into a grin. "Mainly because of his family, especially his nephews. When it became evident that the number of male Westmorelands was increasing and this place would be their summer home, Uncle Corey decided he needed lots of space and a huge food budget."

Madison blinked. "You mean, while growing up, all eleven of you would visit at the same time?"

Stone chuckled. "Yeah, we would all be here at the same time. But you'd better believe that, although everyone thought Uncle Corey was nuts for having all of us here, they knew him well enough to know that he would keep us in line and keep us busy. He did and we loved it. My fondest childhood memories were of the times I spent here. That's why me and my four brothers and six cousins have such a close relationship. Each summer we did some serious male bonding and learned how to get along with each other. Once in a while, we'd let Delaney come with us during the summer, but she preferred coming during her spring breaks."

Madison nodded. "Your uncle must really like kids."

Stone smile wavered some. "He does. It's unfortunate that he never married and had any of his own."

She gazed at him. "Do you like kids?"

He cast her a sideways glance. "Yes. Why do you ask?"

"Because I think it's unfortunate that in a few years you're going to find yourself in the same situation as your uncle."

He held her gaze for a long moment, then said in a low voice, "Yeah, I guess you're right. Come on. Chances are Uncle Corey knows we're coming."

Madison lifted her brow as the horses moved forward at a slow pace with Stone traveling slightly ahead. "How will he know that?"

Stone turned and looked back at her and the chuckle that poured from his lips seemed to echo in the wind. "Because Uncle Corey knows the moment anyone sets foot on his mountain. He may not know it's us who's coming but he knows that somebody is on his property."

And as if to prove how well Stone knew his uncle, Madison watched as the front door of the huge ranch house swung open and a bear of a man—who looked to stand at least six-five—stepped out onto the wraparound porch. He was wearing a Stetson on his head and peered at them as if trying to make out the identity of his trespassers. When moments passed and it became obvious that he'd figured out that at least one of them was his nephew, he smiled, tugged at the brim of his Stetson and stepped off the porch to come and meet them.

When he came closer the first thing Madison saw was that he was definitely a Westmoreland. Upon first meeting Durango she had immediately known that he and Stone were related and the same held true for Corey Westmoreland. He had the same dark eyes, the same forehead, chin and full lips.

The next thing she noticed was that, at fifty-four, he was a very good-looking man. Like his two nephews, he was magnificent. When he removed his hat she saw that his dark hair had streaks of gray at the temple, making him seem distinguished, as well as handsome. And he appeared to be in excellent physical shape. This was definitely a man who could still grab female interest and she could see why her mother had evidently found him attractive and irresistible.

As soon as Corey reached them Stone brought his bay to a stop and was off his horse in a flash, engulfing his uncle in a huge embrace. "Well, my word Stone, it's good seeing you. I almost forgot Durango had mentioned that you would be visiting these parts. The phone's been down for a couple of weeks and I've been cut off from civilization."

Corey Westmoreland then turned his attention to Madison who was still sitting on the back of her horse staring at him. He tipped his hat to her. "Howdy, ma'am," he said walking over and offering her his hand in a friendly handshake. "Welcome to Corey's Mountain and who might you be?"

Madison saw the look of amusement in Corey Westmoreland's dark eyes and knew he had immediately jumped to the conclusion that she was there because of Stone and that the two of them were lovers. She could give him credit for being partly right.

She accepted his assistance when he reached up to help her off her horse and knew the exact moment that Stone came to stand beside her. "Hello, Mr. Westmoreland, I'm Madison Winters and I've come to see my mother."

There was complete silence for a few moments, then Madison watched as the look in Corey Westmoreland's eyes became tender and, when he spoke, his tone of voice matched that look. "So you're Madison? I've heard a lot about you. Abby will be glad to see you."

Madison nodded as she tried reading signs in the older man's features that indicated otherwise. "She doesn't know I'm coming."

He chuckled. "That won't mean a thing. She hoped you had gotten the messages she'd left so you wouldn't worry. With the phones being down, she couldn't leave any more. I'm hoping Liam will be feeling well enough to do the repairs."

Madison lifted a brow. "Liam?"

"Yes, he's another rancher who lives on the opposite mountain. He's also the area's repair man and electrician."

Corey Westmoreland put his hat back on. "But enough about that. I'm sure you're eager to see your mama."

"Yes, I am." Madison glanced around. "Is she still here?" She watched as the man's mouth lit into a huge smile.

"Yes, she's here. Go on up to the house and open the door and go right on in. When I walked out she was in the middle of preparing dinner."

Madison blinked. "Dinner? My mother is actually cooking?"

"Yes."

Madison frowned. She couldn't remember the last time her mother had cooked. She turned to Stone. "Are you coming?"

He shook his head. "I'll be in later. I need to talk to Uncle Corey about something."

She nodded. Although she knew he probably did need to talk to his uncle, she also knew that he was hanging back to give her and her mother time alone. "All right." And without saying anything else, she walked the short distance to the house alone, wondering what she would say to her mother when she saw her.

Madison opened the door and cautiously walked inside the impressive house. She heard the sound of a woman humming and immediately knew it was her mother's voice. Quickly glancing around she scanned her surroundings. The inside of Corey's ranch house was just as huge as the outside. The heavy furnishings were made of rich, supple leather and were durable and made to last forever. The place looked neat and well-lived-in and several vases of fresh flowers denoted a feminine touch.

"Dinner's almost ready, Corey. I think a soak in the hot tub would be nice afterwards, what do you think?"

Madison swallowed as the sound of her mother's voice reached her. Evidently she had heard the door open and assumed it was Corey Westmoreland returning. Sighing deeply, Madison crossed the living room to the kitchen and came to a stop in the doorway. Her mother, the prim-and-proper Abby Winters, was bending over checking something in the oven. She was wearing a pair of jeans, a short top, was barefoot and had her hair untied and flowing down her back. Her mother had always been weight conscious and had a nice figure; the outfit she was wearing clearly showed just how nice that figure was.

Madison blinked, not sure if this sexy looking creature in Corey Westmoreland's kitchen was actually her mother. She looked more like a woman in her thirties than someone who had turned fifty earlier that year. And Madison found it hard to believe that the woman who normally wore conservative business suits, high-heeled pumps and her hair up in a bun was the same person standing less than ten feet away from her.

"Mom?"

Abby Winters snatched her head up and met Madison's uncertain gaze. She blinked, as if making sure she was really seeing her daughter, and then a huge smile touched both corners of her lips and she quickly crossed the room. "Maddy, what are you doing here?" she asked, mere seconds before engulfing Madison in a colossal hug.

"I wanted to make sure you were all right," Madison said when her mother finally released her.

Her mother lifted a worried brow. "Didn't you get my messages saying I was extending my trip?"

"Yes, but I had to see for myself that you were okay."

Abby pulled her daughter back to her. "Oh, sweetheart, I'm sorry that you were worried about me, but I'm fine."

Madison sighed. What she needed to hear was a little more than that, but before she could open her mouth to say anything, she heard the front door open and Stone and Corey Westmoreland walked in. She watched the expression on her mother's face when she looked up and saw Stone's uncle. If there was any doubt in Madison's mind, it vanished with the look the two of them exchanged. It was a good thing they were already in the kitchen because she could certainly feel the heat simmering between them. It was quite obvious that her mother and Corey Westmoreland had a thing going on.

Madison cleared her throat. "Mom, this is Stone, Mr. Westmoreland's nephew and my friend. Stone, this is my mother, Abby Winters."

She saw Stone blink and knew the prim-and-proper picture she had painted of her mother was definitely not the one Stone was seeing. He took a step forward and took Abby's hand in a warm handshake. "Nice meeting you, Ms. Winters."

Abby Winters' smiled warmly. "And it's nice meeting you, Stone. Corey speaks highly of you and I've read every book you've written. You're a gifted author."

"Thank you."

"And please call me Abby." She glanced back at Madison. "How do the two of you know each other?"

"We met on the plane flying out here," Stone said before Madison could respond.

Abby's smile widened. "Oh, how nice. I'm glad that Madison had some company for the flight. I know how much she detests flying."

The room got quiet and then Abby spoke again. "Corey and I were just about to have dinner. He can show you where the two of you can stay and then we'll sit down and eat. I'm sure you must be hungry."

Madison was more curious as to what was going on between her mother and Corey Westmoreland than she was hungry, but decided she and her mother would talk later. That was a definite. "That's fine."

Sighing deeply, she and Stone followed Corey Westmoreland out of the kitchen.

"So you have no idea who's trying to find you, Uncle Corey?" Stone asked later as he stood with his uncle on the porch. Dinner had been wonderful. For someone who Madison thought couldn't cook, her mother had prepared a delicious feast. Madison and her mother were inside doing dishes and no doubt Madison was grilling her mother on her relationship with Corey. As yet, his uncle had not explained anything to him. Corey acted like it was an everyday occurrence for Stone to show up on his mountain and find a woman cooking and serving as hostess as if she had permanent residence there.

Corey leaned against a column post. "No, I don't know a living soul who would be looking for me," he said shaking his head in confusion. "You said Quade is checking things out?"

"Yes. Durango contacted him."

Corey nodded. "Then there's nothing for me to do but

wait until I hear from him." He then looked over at his nephew. "Madison is a pretty thing. She reminds me of Abby when she was young."

Stone turned and gazed at his uncle. "You knew Abby Winters before?"

Corey chuckled as if amused. "Of course. Do you think we just met yesterday?"

Stone shook his head as if to clear his brain. "Hell, Uncle Corey, I didn't know what to think and Madison is even more confused."

Corey nodded again. "I'm sure Abby will explain things to her."

Stone crossed his arms over his chest. "How about if you explain things to me."

A few moments later, Corey sighed deeply. "All right. Let's take a walk."

The two of them walked down a path that Stone remembered well. It was the way to the natural spring that was on his uncle's property. He remembered how he and his brothers and cousins had spent many hours in it having lots of fun. The sun had gone down but it wasn't completely dark yet. The scent of pine filled the air.

"Abby and I met when I was in my last year at Montana State. She had come with her parents to visit Yellowstone as a graduation gift before starting college. I was working part-time at the park and will never forget the day I saw her. She was barely eighteen and I thought I had died and gone to heaven. When I finally got the chance to talk to her without her parents around, I knew she was the person I had fallen in love with and someone I would never forget." Corey smiled. "And she felt the same way.

It was love at first sight and the attraction between us was spontaneous."

The smile then vanished from Corey's face. "It was also forbidden love because she was about to become engaged to another man, someone attending Harvard. He was a man her well-to-do family had picked out for her, one of those affairs where two families get together and decide their kids will marry. And no matter how we felt about each other I knew Abby wouldn't change her mind. She was raised not to defy her parents. Besides, I was not in a position to ask her to stay with me. Her fiancé's family had money and I barely had a job. When she left I never saw her again and she took my heart with her. I knew then that I would never marry, because the one woman I wanted was lost to me forever."

Stone nodded, wondering how he would feel if the one woman he wanted was lost to him forever. "There was never another woman over the years that you grew to love?"

Corey shook his head. "No. There was one woman I took up with a year or two later, when I worked for a while as a ranger in the Tennessee Mountains. I tried to make things work with her, but couldn't. We stayed together for almost a year but she knew my heart belonged to someone else. And one day she just took off and I haven't seen her since."

Stone nodded again. "So when you saw Abby three weeks ago, that was the first time the two of you had seen each other in over thirty-two years?"

Corey smiled. "Yes, and we recognized each other immediately and the spark was still there. And after a few hours of conversations—she told me her life story and I told her mine—we decided to do what we couldn't do then, all those years ago. Steal away and be alone. After talking to her it was plain to see she had lived a lonely life just like I had, and we felt we owed it to each other to start enjoying life to the fullest and to be happy. She's only been here three weeks but Abby has brought nothing but joy and happiness to my life, Stone. I can't imagine my life without her now and she's assured me that she feels the same way."

Stone stopped walking and stared at his uncle. "What are you saying?"

A huge grin spread across Corey Westmoreland's face. "I've asked Abby to marry me and she's accepted."

Madison stared at her mother in shock. "Marriage? You and Corey Westmoreland?"

Abby smiled at her only child as she handed her a dish to dry. "Yes. He asked and I accepted. Corey and I met and fell in love the year before I entered Harvard. My parents had already decided my future was with your father and I was the obedient daughter who wouldn't defy their plans."

Madison continued to stare at her mother. "So I assumed right. You and Dad never loved each other."

Abby reached out and took her daughter's hand in hers, knowing that Madison was probably confused by a lot of things. "In a way, your father and I did love each other but not the way I loved Corey. As long as your father was alive, I was determined to make our marriage work, and I did. I was faithful to your father, Madison, and I was a good wife."

Madison knew that was true. "So you came out here hoping that you'd run into Corey Westmoreland again?"

Abby smiled as she shook her head. "No. For all I knew Corey had gotten on with his life and was married with a bunch of kids. I knew he had wanted to become a park ranger, but I didn't even know if he still lived in this area. Imagine my shock when I went out to dinner that night and he walked into the restaurant. He looked at me and I looked at him and it was as if the years hadn't mattered. I knew then that I still loved him and I also knew that the most joyous part of my life was the summer I met him."

Her hand tightened on Madison's. "But that doesn't mean your father didn't bring me joy. It means that with Corey I can be someone I could never be with your father."

In a way Madison understood. During the past two days, she had behaved in ways with Stone that she had never behaved with Cedric. "So when is the wedding?"

"In a few months. We decided to wait until after his nephew Thorn's next race. That way Corey can make the announcement to all of his family at one time. The entire Westmoreland family always attends Thorn's races."

Madison sighed deeply. "What about you? What about your life back in Boston?"

Abby smiled. "I plan to keep Abby's Manor since there's definitely a need for day-care facilities for the elderly. And it will continue to be managed the same way it's being managed now. Everything else I can tie up rather quickly. My friends, if they are truly my friends and love me, they will want me to be happy. I haven't been involved with anyone since your father's death over ten years ago. I'm hoping everyone will understand my need to be with him."

She then stared for a long moment at her daughter.

"What about you, Madison? You are the person who concerns me the most. Do you understand?"

Madison met her mother's gaze. Yes, she understood how it felt to want to be happy, mainly because she also knew how it felt to be in love. As unusual as it seemed, her mother still loved Corey Westmoreland after all these years. Their love had been strong enough to withstand more than thirty years of separation. She knew her mother was waiting for her answer. She also knew that her response was important to her. Abby Winters had been right. The people who truly loved her would understand her need to be happy.

Madison reached out and hugged her mother. "Yes, Mom, I understand and I'm happy for you. If marrying Corey Westmoreland makes you happy, then I am happy."

Abby's arms tightened around her daughter. "Thank you, sweetheart."

Stone Westmoreland glanced at the clock on the nightstand next to the bed. It was after midnight and he couldn't sleep. He had Madison on his mind. She and her mother had joined him and Uncle Corey on the porch and she had congratulated his uncle on his upcoming marriage to her mother and had even gone a step further and hugged Uncle Corey and welcomed him to the family. Uncle Corey had done likewise and welcomed her to his. Then Madison had indicated to all that she was tired and would be going to bed early. He of all people knew of her overabundance of energy and figured that it wasn't exhaustion that had made her escape to her room. She was trying to come to terms with her mother's marriage announcement.

Getting out of bed he slipped into his jeans. Quietly opening the door he entered the darkened hallway. He had walked this hallway many times and knew his way around, even in the dark. The room Madison had been given was only a couple of doors from his. He wondered how she felt knowing his uncle and her mother were probably sharing a bed tonight. He doubted they would change their routine because of their unexpected guests, especially since they intended to marry.

He opened the door and quietly slipped into Madison's bedroom. As soon as he entered and closed the door behind him, he saw her. She was standing across the room gazing out of the window. From where he stood he saw she was wearing a nightgown and the light from the moon that shone through the window silhouetted how the sleepwear sensuously draped her figure.

He breathed in deeply. As much as he wanted her, he hadn't come to her for that. He wanted to hold her in his arms because whether she admitted it or not, she *was* having a problem coming to terms with her mother's upcoming marriage to his uncle.

"Madison." He whispered the name softly and she quickly turned around.

"Stone?"

Without answering, he quickly crossed the room and pulled her into his arms and kissed her, needing the taste of her and wanting to give her the taste of him. Her response made him deepen the kiss and when his tongue took control of hers, the soft moans that flowed from deep within her throat nearly pushed him over the edge.

He gently broke off the kiss. "You were quiet after dinner. Are you all right?"

She nodded against his chest and his arms around her tightened. "They are happy together, Madison," he said, trying to reassure her.

She pulled back from him and glanced up. "I know that, Stone, and that's what's so sad. They went all those years loving each other but not being able to be together."

Stone nodded. "Yeah, my uncle told me."

Madison sighed. "They fell in love from the first. According to Mom, she fell in love with your uncle the first time she saw him although she knew her life was destined to be with someone else."

Stone stared down at her for a moment then asked, "And how do you feel about that, Madison?"

She knew why he was asking. The man her mother had married instead of Corey Westmoreland had been her father. "My heart aches for the three of them. What if there was someone who my father would have preferred to love. I think it's ridiculous for parents to plan their children's future that way. I won't ever do that to my kids."

Stone had been rubbing her back. He suddenly paused. "Kids? You plan to have kids?"

She looked up at him and smiled. "Yes, one day."

He nodded. That meant she also planned on getting married one day. Hellfire. He sure didn't like the thought of that. "You need to get into bed and try and get some sleep."

He saw awareness flash in her eyes when she suddenly realized he wasn't wearing a shirt. "I'll only get into bed if you get in with me."

He shook his head. "With your mother and Uncle Corey at the end of the hall, I don't think that's a good idea." He didn't want to bring up the fact that he doubted he could lie beside her for any period of time without wanting to make love to her, and their lovemaking tended to be rather noisy.

"Please. I promise to behave. Just stay with me for a little while."

He looked down at her and knew she had no intention of behaving. He would stay but would somehow dredge up enough control to behave for the both of them. "All right, into bed you go. I'll stay with you for a little while."

"Thanks, Stone."

He walked her over to the bed and pushed the covers aside. She slid in and he slid in beside her and pulled her into his arms. She automatically shifted her body in a spoon position against him and he knew she felt his arousal through his jeans. "Wouldn't you be more comfortable if you were to take off your pants?" she asked in a soft voice.

He tightened his arms around her. "Go to sleep, Madison," he growled in her ear.

"Are you sure you want me to do that?"

"Yes, I'm sure. Now go to sleep." He knew he didn't want her to do that but under the circumstances he had no choice. He hadn't missed the looks his uncle had given him at dinner. Corey and Abby were curious about his relationship with Madison. Although they hadn't asked anything, they had gone quiet when Madison had innocently mentioned they had stayed at the Quinns' cabin for two days.

A few hours later, the only sounds Stone heard were Madison's soft even breathing and a coyote that was howling in the distance. He leaned over and kissed her lips then slipped from the bed to return to his room. Before opening the door he glanced back over to look at her and knew that, if he had been in his uncle's shoes thirty some years ago and Madison had been her mother, there was no way he would have let her go and marry another man.

There was no way on God's green earth that he would have allowed that to happen.

Nine

The next two weeks flew by and Madison's heart swelled each and every time she saw her mother and Corey Westmoreland interacting together. It was quite obvious the two were in love and were making up for lost time. She had never seen her mother smile so much and it seemed that Corey had brought out a totally different woman in Abby Winters. Her mother enjoyed cooking, baking and thought nothing of helping Corey do chores around the ranch.

The days of the prim-and-proper Abby Winters were over—but not completely. She still set the table like she was expecting guests for dinner and occasionally Madison would hear classical music on the disc player. Madison liked the change in her mother and more and more she was accepting Corey's role in her life.

Madison then thought about her own love life or lack

of it. Stone still came to her room every night and held her until she went off to sleep. In respect for her mother and his uncle, he refused to make love to her although she always tried tempting him into doing so.

She had looked forward to today. Her mother and Corey had mentioned a few days ago that they would be gone from the ranch most of the day to visit another rancher who lived on the other side of the mountain. That meant that she and Stone would have the entire house to themselves and she intended to make good use of it.

She was aware that it had been hard for him to keep his hands off her and it had been just as hard for her to keep her hands off him. All it took was a look across the table into his dark eyes to see the longing and desire, and to know what he was thinking and feel the sexual currents that radiated from his gaze.

He stayed away from the house most of the day helping his uncle do various chores around the ranch. Corey had decided that, with Stone there, now was a good time to start constructing a new barn. When Stone came in each afternoon he would take a bath before dinner and usually retired to his room to work on his book after sitting and talking with everyone for a while. But no matter how tired he was, he always came to her room every night to spend time with her. They would sometimes sit and talk for hours. He would tell her about the book he was working on and the scenes he had plotted that day. Once or twice he even read some of them to her and she was amazed how his mind worked to come up with some of the stuff he'd written.

Madison sighed with disappointment as she sat at the kitchen table and looked out. It seemed that she and Stone wouldn't have the ranch to themselves today after all. Corey had announced at breakfast that he and Abby had changed their minds and would visit the Monroes another time. She had glanced across the table and seen the same disappointment in Stone's eyes that she knew had been in hers.

"It's a beautiful day for a picnic, don't you think?"

She glanced around and met her mother's smiling face, then shrugged her shoulders. "I suppose so."

"Then why don't you find Stone and suggest that the two of you go to Cedar Canyon? You can take the SUV and not worry about traveling by horseback. It's simply beautiful and there's a lake so you may want to take your bathing suit with you."

Madison perked up. The picnic sounded nice, but... "I don't have a bathing suit."

Abby chuckled. "You can certainly borrow one of mine. That's one of the first things Corey made sure I had when I came here. With so many hot springs and lakes around, it would be a waste not to have one."

Madison glanced back out of the window. She saw Stone in the distance standing next to the corral gate as he watched his uncle rope a calf. "Stone may be too busy to want to take off like that."

Abby chuckled again. "Oh, I don't know. Something tells me that he'll like the idea."

Stone definitely liked the idea and when Madison suggested it he didn't waste any time going into the house to shower and change. He was dying to be alone with her away from the ranch. And the way he was driving the truck indicated that he was in a rush to get to their destination.

"We will get there in one piece won't we, Stone?"

He glanced over at Madison and even though she was smiling, she was hinting that he slow down. He had made a couple of sharp turns around several curves. "Sorry. I guess I'm kind of eager to get there."

She gave him an innocent look. "Why? Are you hungry? Is what's in that picnic basket tempting you?"

He met her gaze and decided to be completely honest. "Yes, I'm hungry but my hunger has nothing to do with what's in that damn basket. You're what's tempting me. Aren't you?" He watched the smile that spread across her lips; lips he was dying to kiss. He had noticed each and every time she had inched her skirt up her legs, although he should have been keeping his eyes on the road.

"Yes. I just wanted to make sure you wanted me," she said grinning.

He brought the car to a screeching stop. Taking a deep breath, he turned to face her. "I want you, Madison, don't doubt that. I want you so bad that I ache. I want you so bad that if I don't get inside of you real soon, I might embarrass myself."

She glanced down at his midsection and nodded when she saw what he meant. "Then I guess we'd better be on our way again, because I wouldn't want that to happen."

"No."

She lifted a brow. "No?"

"No, I don't think I can wait now."

Her brow lifted when she saw he was unbuttoning his shirt. He removed it and tossed it in the back seat of the SUV. She swallowed hard. She had seen him shirtless numerous times but still her midsection filled with heat each and every time she saw him that way. And she didn't want to think about how turned on she got whenever she saw him naked.

"Uhh, would you like to tell me what's going on here?" she said in a low voice. Desire was making it almost impossible for her to speak.

His smile widened into a grin. It was a smile so hot she felt heat center between her legs in reaction to it. "We're what's going on. And the one thing I really like about this SUV is that it's very roomy. My brother Dare owns one and he let my brother Storm borrow it when his car was in the shop. He later wished that he hadn't. Storm discovered just how roomy it was when he used it to go out on a date."

Stone chuckled as he shook his head. "Needless to say, Dare learned his lesson when he found a pair of women's panties under the seat the next day and he swore never to let Storm borrow his truck again."

Madison grinned. "Sounds like your brother Storm is quite a character."

"Yeah, for some reason the women think so and around Atlanta he's known as 'The Perfect Storm.' Of course none of us think there's anything perfect about him but evidently the women do. I don't know who's worse, him or Durango."

After unzipping his jeans, he lifted his hips to pull them off. Madison, he noticed, was watching him intently. "Instead of paying so much attention to me, you might want to start stripping."

She blinked in pure innocence. "Surely you're not suggesting that I get naked?"

"Yeah, that's exactly what I'm suggesting since seeing you naked is definitely one of my fantasies today. I want you naked and stretched out beneath me. Then I want to get inside you and stroke you until you can't take any more," he whispered huskily across the cab of the vehicle.

Madison swallowed. Her heart began pounding. The heat between her legs broke out into a flame. She began burning everywhere, but especially there. "Okay, you've convinced me to cooperate," she said, lifting her shirt and pulling down her panties. She held the strap of black lace up in her hand. "I need to make sure I put these back on. I don't want your uncle to find these in his truck like your brother Dare found those in his."

Stone reached out and plucked them out of her hand and stuffed them in the pocket of his jeans before pulling out a pack of condoms. "I'll try to remember to give them back to you," he said grinning. He then tossed his jeans in the back seat to join his shirt. He glanced over at her. "Need help removing that skirt and blouse?"

Madison smiled. "No thanks. I think I can manage."

"All right." And he got an eyeful while he saw her doing so. He was glad she hadn't needed his help. In his present state he might have been tempted to rip her clothes right off her. His breath caught when he saw she hadn't worn a bra and, when she removed her top, her breasts spilled free and his shaft reacted by getting even harder.

Madison glanced over at Stone. God, she wanted him. Bad. All his talk about wanting her and needing to get inside of her and stroking her had set her on fire. And she didn't feel a moment of embarrassment sitting with him naked in the truck. She was beginning to discover that with Stone she could be prim and proper and she could also be bad and naughty. She felt him ease the bench-seat back and the SUV became roomier.

She licked her lips when she gazed down at him—especially a certain part of him. "And you're sure no one will surprise us and come along?" There was a husky tone to her voice that even she didn't recognize.

"Yeah, I'm sure. I'd never risk exposing you like that. I intend to be the only man ever to see you naked."

She opened her mouth to tell him that sounded pretty much like a declaration that he intended to be with her for a while, but before she could get the words out he had captured her mouth in his and pulled her across the seat to him.

His kiss reflected all the want and desire he'd claimed he had for her; all that he'd been holding back for the past weeks. Now he was letting go and the moan that erupted deep in her throat was letting him know that she appreciated it.

She had missed this, a chance to moan and groan to her heart's delight without having to worry about anyone hearing her. But she knew that Stone had something else in store for her, too. Today he intended to make her scream.

In a smooth and swift move, he had her on her back and the leather felt warm against her naked back and his body felt hot to her naked front. And then there was that hard part of him that was insistently probing trying to get inside of her. She decided the least she could do—since she was more than eager for this pleasure—was to help him along. She reached out and held him in her hand. He felt hot, hard and thick.

"Take it home, baby."

Stone's words, whispered in a deep, husky tone, sent

sensuous chills all through her body and she adjusted her body when he lifted her hips to place her legs on his shoulders. She guided him home and when he entered her and went deep, his growl of pleasure mingled with her sigh of contentment.

He gazed down at her and the look of desire in his eyes touched her in a way she had never been touched. He smiled and so did she. "I know this vehicle is roomy, now let's see how sturdy it is."

Before she could figure out what he meant he began thrusting inside of her at a rhythm that had her groaning and moaning. The seat rocked and she thought she felt the entire truck shake as his body melded into hers over and over again.

"I can't get enough of you, Madison," he groaned throatily as he continued to mate with her, stunned by the degree of wanting and desire he had for her. His jaw clenched and he hissed through his teeth when he felt her muscles tighten around him mercilessly. He reacted by thrusting into her even more. He felt her body shudder and when she let out a scream that was loud enough to send the wildlife scattering for miles, he threw his head back as his own body exploded. At that very moment he thought that he had to be stone crazy, especially when he felt another orgasm rip through her.

"Damn!" Never had he felt such a mind-blowing experience. It was a wonder the truck hadn't flipped over. The windows had definitely gotten steamy.

Moments later they collapsed in each other arms. Stone raised his head to gaze down at the woman still beneath him; the woman he was still intimately connected to; the woman he wanted again already. And he knew without a doubt that he wasn't stone crazy, but he was stone in love.

"So how was the picnic?" Corey asked as he sat down to the kitchen table for dinner.

"It was nice," Madison quickly said, glancing across the table to Stone. She was glad he didn't lift his head to look at her because if he'd done so, it would definitely have given something away. After making love in the truck a second time, they had continued on to Cedar Canyon. They spread a blanket next to the lake and ate the delicious snack her mother had packed for them. Then they had undressed and made love again on the blanket before going swimming. Then they had made love several more times before coming back to the ranch. To say the picnic had been nice was putting it mildly.

After dinner the four of them were sitting on the porch listening to Corey talk about the progress he and Stone were making on the barn, when one of the dogs barked. Corey glanced in the distance and saw riders approaching.

"Looks like we have visitors," he said, standing. He used his hand as a shield as he squinted the brilliance of the evening sun from his eyes. A smile touched his lips when he said, "It looks like Quade and Durango, and they have two other men with them."

Everyone watched the riders approach. Madison blinked when she saw the men, surprised that Corey didn't recognize the other two since it was crystal clear all of them were Westmorelands. The four could pass for brothers. She glanced over at Stone, but he was looking at the other two men intently, as well. The four riders dismounted and walked toward the porch.

"Durango, Quade, good seeing you," Corey said, grabbing his nephews in bear hugs. He then turned to the other two men. "I'm Corey Westmoreland and welcome to Corey's Mountain." He then frowned, as if seeing them had him confused. He stared at them for a second. "Do I know you two? Damn, I hate staring, but the two of you look a hell of a lot like my nephews here."

Quade Westmoreland cleared his throat. "There's a reason for that Uncle Corey."

Corey glanced over at Quade and lifted a brow. "There is?"

"Yes," Durango said quietly. "I'm sure Stone told you that someone was looking for you."

Corey nodded. "Yeah, that's what I heard. So what has that to do with these two?"

When everyone went silent, Corey crossed his arms over his chest. "Okay, what the hell is going on?"

One of the men, the taller of the two, spoke up. "Do you remember a Carolyn Roberts?"

Corey's arms dropped to his side. "Yes, I remember Carolyn. Why? What is she to you?"

The other man, who was just as tall as Corey, then spoke. "She was our mother."

"Was?" Corey asked softly.

"Yes, she died six months ago."

Corey shook his head sadly as he remembered the woman he'd dated a full year before they'd gone their separate ways, never to see each other again. "I'm sorry to hear that and you have my condolences. Your mother was a good woman."

"And she told us just moments before she died that you were a good man," the taller of the two said.

Corey sighed deeply. "I appreciate her thinking that way."

"That's not all Mrs. Roberts told them, Uncle Corey. I think you need to hear the rest of it," Quade Westmoreland said.

After glancing over at his nephew, Corey turned to the men. "All right. What else did she tell you?"

The two men looked from one to the other before the taller answered. "She also told us that we were your sons."

It was evident that the two men's statement had shaken Corey, Madison thought. But then all you had to do was to look at the other three Westmorland nephews to know their claim was true. Quade was a good-looking man and reminded her a lot of Stone. He was quiet and didn't say much, but when he spoke people listened. And there was a dangerous look about him like he enjoyed living on the edge and wouldn't hesitate to take anything into his own hands if the need arose. Then there were the other two men, who until a few minutes ago were virtual strangers. The only names they'd given were their first ones, Clint and Cole. They said they would explain everything once they were seated at the table where they could talk.

Now it seemed everyone was ready. Her mother, being the ever-gracious and proper hostess, had made coffee and served Danishes when the men declined dinner. Abby was now seated beside Corey and, understanding her mother's presence but thinking this was a family matter and her presence wasn't warranted, Madison was about to leave to go to her room when Stone grabbed her arm and almost tugged her down in his lap. "Stay," he said so close to her lips she thought he was going to kiss her.

She glanced over at his cousin Quade who smiled mysteriously. She looked at Stone and nodded, "All right," and sat down in the chair beside him.

"Now, will the two of you start from the beginning?" Corey Westmoreland asked Clint and Cole.

Clint, the taller of the two men began speaking. "Twenty-nine years ago Carolyn gave birth to triplets and—"

"Triplets!" Corey exclaimed, nearly coming out of his seat.

Clint nodded. "Yes."

Corey shook his head. "Multiple births run in this family, but…hell, I didn't even know she was pregnant."

"Yes, she said she left without telling you after the two of you broke up. She moved to Beaumont, Texas, where an aunt and uncle lived. She showed up on their doorstep and fabricated the story that she had married a man who'd been a rodeo bronco and that he'd gotten killed while competing. She claimed that man's name was Corey Westmoreland and she was the widowed Carolyn Westmoreland. She'd even obtained false papers to prove it. We can only assume she did that because she was twenty-four and her aunt and uncle, her only relatives, were deeply religious. They wouldn't look down on her if she told them she was married instead of a girl having a child out of wedlock."

A few moments later Clint continued. "Anyway, she found out she was having triplets and, since she was using the Westmoreland name, the three of us were born as Westmorelands and no questions were asked. We were raised believing our father had died before we were born and never thought any differently until Mom called us in just seconds before she passed away and told us the truth."

Cole took up the story. "She said our father was Corey Westmoreland but he wasn't dead like she'd told us over the years. She said she didn't know where you were and would leave it up to us to find you. She told us to tell you, when we did find you, that she was sorry for not letting you know about us. If she had told you about her pregnancy she thought you would have done the honorable thing and married her, although she knew you didn't love her and that your heart still belonged to another. We promised her just seconds before her eyes closed that we would do what we could to find you and deliver that message. I believe that she was able to die in peace after that."

For a long moment no one at the table said anything and Madison felt the exact moment Stone took her hand in his and held it like the story had touched him deeply. She understood. It had touched her, as well.

Corey Westmoreland cleared his throat but everyone could see the tears that misted his eyes. "I thank her for wanting me to know the truth after all these years." He then cleared his throat again. "You said there were triplets. Does that mean there's a third one of you?"

A smile touched Clint's lips. "Yes, I'm technically the oldest, Cole's in the middle and Casey is the last."

Corey Westmoreland swallowed deeply. "I have three sons?"

Clint chuckled as he shook his head. "No, you have two sons. Casey is a girl and, just so you know, the reason she's not here is because she's having a hard time dealing with all of this. She and Mom were close and for years she thought you were dead and now to discover you're alive and that Mom kept it from us has her going through some changes right now."

Once again there was silence at the table and then Stone spoke. "Damn, another Westmoreland girl and we thought Delaney was the only one." He turned and smiled at the two men, his newfound cousins. "Delaney is my sister and we thought she was the only female in the Westmoreland family in this generation. Did the two of you catch hell being big brothers to Casey as much as my four brothers and six cousins caught hell looking out for Delaney?"

Clint and Cole exchanged huge grins. "Hell wasn't all we caught being brothers to Casey. Wait until you meet her, then you'll understand why."

Madison cuddled closer into Stone's embrace as they lay in bed together. "In a way, today's event had a happy ending to a rather sad beginning. At least Clint and Cole got to meet Corey and Corey found out he had two sons and a daughter."

"Umm," Stone said, placing a kiss on Madison's lips. "Uncle Corey is going to make history in the Westmoreland family. He'll become a father and a groom within months of each other. He was so excited that he picked up the phone to call everyone but then remembered the phone was dead. I can't wait until the family gets the news." He chuckled. "And when Clint and Cole told Uncle Corey what they did for a living, he was as proud as could be." Both Clint and Cole were Texas Rangers. According to the brothers, Casey owned a clothing store in Beaumont.

Less than an hour later, when Madison had fallen asleep, Stone slipped out of her bedroom and ran smack into Durango. Durango placed his arms across his chest and had a smirk on his face. "Making late night visits, I see."

Stone frowned. "You see too much, Durango? Why aren't you in bed like everyone else."

"Because, Cuz, I was looking for you. When you weren't in your room I assumed you had gone outside to take a dip in the hot spring. Evidently I was wrong."

Stone glared at him. "Evidently. Now why were you looking for me?"

Durango reached into his pocket and pulled out an envelope. "To give you this. I almost forgot because of the excitement. This telegram came for you a few days ago. I assume it might be important."

Stone took the envelope from Durango, tore it open and scanned the contents. "Damn!"

Durango lifted a brow. "Bad news?"

Stone shook his head. "It's from my agent. I sold another book and the offer is eight figures and a Hollywood studio has bought an option on it. He wants me in New York in two days to announce everything at the Harlem Book Fair."

Durango smiled. "Hey, Stone, that's wonderful news and I'd think announcing the deal at that book fair would be good publicity."

"Yeah, but I don't want to go anywhere right now."

Durango lifted a dark brow in confusion. "Why not?" When Stone didn't respond he said. "Oh, I see."

Stone frowned. "And just what do you see, Durango?"

"I see that a city girl has wrapped herself around your

heart like one wrapped herself around mine a few years ago. Take my advice and be careful about falling in love. Heartache is one hell of a pain to bear."

Stone sighed deeply as he met his cousin's gaze. "Your advice comes too late, Durango. I think I'm already there." Without saying anything else, he walked off.

Stone glanced at his watch as he waited for Madison to come to breakfast the next morning. He would be leaving with Durango and Quade when they left in less than an hour. Clint and Cole would be staying awhile to spend time with Corey and Abby.

"Stone? Mom said you wanted to see me."

Stone glanced up and smiled when he saw Madison enter the room. She was dressed in a pair of jeans and a Western shirt and looked feminine as hell. He took her hand in his. "Durango gave me a telegram last night. My agent wants me in New York for an important media announcement regarding a recent book deal. I need to leave for New York as soon as possible."

Madison's features filled with disappointment. "Oh." Then, after taking a deep breath, she met his gaze and said, "I'm going to miss you."

He pulled her into his arms. "I'm going to miss you, too. I'll be back as soon as it's over. Will you be here when I return?"

She met his gaze. "I'm not sure, Stone, I—"

"Please stay until I get back, Madison. You haven't been to Yellowstone and I'd like to take you there."

She smiled. "I think I'd like that."

Not caring who might walk up on them at any moment,

he pulled her into his arms and kissed her deeply, needing to take the taste of her with him and wanting to leave the taste of him with her. He planned for them to have a long talk about their future when he returned.

"I'll be back as soon as I can," he whispered against her moist lips.

She nodded. "I'll be counting the days."

He pulled her closer into his arms. "So will I."

Ten

At any other time Stone would have enjoyed attending a gala thrown in his honor, but at this moment he didn't appreciate that his agent, Weldon Harris, had planned the surprise event. Even the media had been invited and he cringed when he saw that the one reporter he detested, Noreen Baker, was among the crowd.

He was even more mad that what was supposed to have been a weekend affair in New York had stretched into a full week including unscheduled interviews and parties that his agent had arranged for him to attend. He hated that his uncle's phone still wasn't working. He had no way to let Madison know why he hadn't returned to the mountains.

He saw Noreen Baker glance his way and knew an encounter with her was the last thing he wanted. He turned to make his escape, but when she called out to him, he decided it would be rude not to acknowledge her. He sighed deeply when she approached.

"Congratulations on your achievements. You must be proud of yourself."

"I am," he said curtly, deciding not to engage in small talk.

She glanced around. "And I must say that this is a real nice party for the prolific Rock Mason."

"I'm glad you like it, Noreen. Now if you will ex—"

"Are you still trying to be a recluse?"

He had turned around to leave but her question ticked him off. "I've never tried to be a recluse. If you would catch me when I'm doing my Teach the People to Read functions you would know that. Instead you prefer attending those affairs that promote dirt instead of positive functions."

Noreen looked at him and smiled. "How about telling me something that's positive?"

"Try doing an article on the Teach the People to Read program."

"No, I want to do an article about you. After the announcement a few days ago, you are definitely big news and being young, single and rich, you will be in demand with the ladies. Any love interests? What about marriage plans?"

Stone immediately thought about Madison. He would gladly announce to the world that she was the woman he loved and the one woman he wanted to marry, but information like that in this particular barracuda's hand might be hurtful to Madison. Noreen would never give her a moment's rest in the process of fishing for a story. She would camp outside Madison's home if it meant getting a scoop.

"How can I consider marriage when there's no special woman in my life?"

Noreen's lips quirked. "What about a special man?"

Stone narrowed his eyes. "You've kept up with my past history long enough to know better than to ask that."

"Okay, so that was a cheap shot and I admit it. So are you telling me that there's no woman that Rock Mason is interested in at the moment? There is no woman you would consider marrying?"

Stone frowned. "I think I've made myself clear on several occasions that Rock Mason enjoys the freedom of being a bachelor too much."

"Is that why you've agreed to do that four-month promotional tour in Europe?"

Stone frowned again, wondering how news of that got leaked to the press. He hadn't made a decision on whether or not he would go on that damn tour and he had told his agent that. A lot depended on Madison. He would only go if she went with him. He had no intention of leaving the woman he loved behind.

He met Noreen's curious gaze and said, "No comment. Now if you will excuse me, there's someone over there that I need to see." Stone then walked off.

Three days later Stone was in his hotel room, finally packing to return to Montana. He had spoken with his family in Atlanta several times over the past week. They had heard from Quade and were excited that there were now three additional Westmorelands. He had also spoken with Durango who indicated that he hadn't seen or spoken to Corey since he'd left.

Stone was anxious to get back to Madison. He missed her like hell. He glanced over at the television when he

heard his name and stopped what he was doing as Noreen
Baker's face appeared on the screen during a segment of
Entertainment Tonight. He crossed the room to turn up the
volume.

"As we reported last week, national bestselling author
Rock Mason accepted an eight-figure deal from Hammond
Publishers and with it came movie options, as well as a
four-month book tour in Europe. I spoke with Rock a few
nights ago at a New York bash given in his honor and he
squashed any rumors that he is romantically involved with
anyone, and went on to assure me that he still prefers bedding women to wedding them. He also plans to leave for
Europe in a few weeks. So any of you women out there
who're holding out for the attention of Mr. Money Maker
himself, don't waste your time. Rock Mason is as hard as
they come when the discussion of marriage comes up and
he intends to maintain his bachelor status for quite a while."

Stone switched off the television, shaking his head. Of
course, as usual, Noreen had reported only part of the truth.
At the moment he hadn't made a decision about Europe.
And of course she had put her own spin on what she had
gleaned from their conversation.

He crossed the room to finish packing. The cab would
be arriving shortly to take him to the airport. Right now the
only thing on his mind was getting back to Madison.

Hundreds of miles away, Madison was also packing. She
had watched *Entertainment Tonight* and had heard everything the reporter had said. Stone had been gone for ten
days and she hadn't heard from him. Although the phone
lines were down, if he had wanted to contact her he could

have sent her a letter or something. The postal plane delivered mail to the residents in the area at least twice a week.

He still prefers bedding women to wedding them…

She closed her eyes, fighting back tears. Why had she allowed things to get serious with Stone when he had told her from the very beginning what his feelings were on the subject of marriage? He didn't want to be accountable for anyone but himself and he was going to prove it by taking off to Europe for the next four months. Any pain she was suffering was nobody's fault but her own so she couldn't feel betrayed in any way. He had been totally upfront and truthful with her. She had been the one to assume she had meant something to him and that each time they'd made love it meant more than just having sex. She had actually thought that—

"You're leaving?"

She turned at the sound of her mother's voice. After meeting her mother's gaze and nodding, she continued packing. Her mother and Corey had been in the living room with her when *ET* had come on and had also heard everything the reporter had said.

"Running away won't solve anything, Madison. You told Stone you would be here when he returned and—"

"What makes you think he's going to return, Mom? You heard what that lady said. He's made plans to do a book tour in Europe. I made a mistake and put too much stock into what I thought he and I were sharing. End of story."

Abby crossed the room and took her daughter's hand in hers. "It's never the end of the story when you love someone. The end of the story only comes when the two of you are together."

Madison pulled her hand from her mother. "That may have worked for you and Corey, but then the two of you love each other and deserve a happy ending. I know how I feel about Stone but at no time did he ever tell me that he loved me, and at no time did he lead me to believe we had a future together. I made a mistake by assuming too much. I never expected to fall in love with him so quickly and so hard, Mom, but I did. Even now I don't regret loving him. The only thing I regret is that he doesn't love me back, but I'll get over it. I'm a survivor, and someway, somehow, I'll eventually forget him."

Abby reached out and pulled Madison into her arms. She knew that now was not a good time to tell her daughter that she knew from firsthand experience a woman could never truly forget the man she loved. She'd been there, had tried doing that and it hadn't worked.

She sighed as she released Madison and stepped back. "So, when do you plan to leave?"

"In the morning. I've already talked to Corey and he said the postal plane will arrive tomorrow with the mail and he's sure they won't mind giving me a lift down the mountain and back to the Silver Arrow ranch. When I get back to Boston I'm going to contact the Institute about helping to provide students with summer lessons."

Abby reached out and stroked her daughter's cheek gently, feeling her pain. For her to even think about getting on a small plane showed how desperate she was to leave. "I had hoped you would stay with Corey and me for a while, at least until the end of the summer."

Madison nodded. She had hoped that, too, but knew the best thing for her was to return to Boston. School would start soon and she would go and get prepared for that. "I'll be back in December for you and Corey's wedding."

Even thinking about that brought her pain, knowing Stone would probably be there for the wedding, too. He would just have returned from Europe. "Besides, you did say you're coming home for a while in September to take care of business matters."

Abby smiled. "And when I do, we'll have to do a play or something. Definitely a concert."

Madison smiled through her tears. "That would be nice, Mom. That will really be nice."

"What do you mean she's not here?"

Corey Westmoreland crossed his arms over his chest and met his nephew's glare. "I mean just what I said. She's not here. Did you actually expect her to stick around after what she heard on that television show?"

Stone frowned. "What television show?"

Corey's frown matched Stone's. "The one where that reporter announced to the whole world that you preferred sleeping with women instead of marrying them. I guess Madison felt she fell within that category."

Frustration racked Stone's body and he rubbed his hand down his face. "How could she think something like that?"

Corey leaned back against the porch's column post. "Why wouldn't she think something like that? Have you ever told her anything different?"

Stone inhaled deeply. "No."

"Well, then. She acted just like any woman would act considering the circumstances. And that reporter also mentioned you had agreed to do some European tour and I guess Madison figured if you were planning to do that then she didn't mean a damn thing to you."

Stone met his uncle's stare. "Madison means everything to me. I love her so much I ache."

Corey rubbed his chin as he eyed his nephew. "And what about all that talk you've done over the years about wanting to have your freedom, seeking adventure and not being responsible for anyone but yourself? Not to mention your fear of losing control of your life?"

"My views on all that changed when I fell in love with Madison."

For the longest moment neither man spoke, then Stone said. "There's no need for me to unpack since I'm leaving as soon as I can grab something to eat."

"Where're you going?"

Stone felt his pocket where he'd placed the diamond ring that he had purchased before leaving New York. "I'm going after Madison."

Stone saw her the moment she came out of the Hoffman Music Institute and began walking down the sidewalk. Abby had told him that, since Madison lived only a few blocks from her school, she preferred walking to work on nice days instead of driving. Besides, on any given day, parking in downtown Boston was known to be limited, as well as expensive.

Today was a fair day. The wind was brisk but the sun overhead added a ray of beauty to the city on the Charles; the city that was the origin of the American Revolution and where buildings, parks, fields and churches echoed the city's patriotic past. He remembered Madison once saying how much she loved Boston and he would gladly make this place his home if that's where she wanted to be. He would move anywhere just as long as they were together.

His heart swelled with love when he continued to watch as she came to Downtown Crossing with its brick streets. He wondered if she intended to go into Macy's and decided that now was the time to make his presence known. He hurriedly crossed the street when she stopped to admire the fruit on display at a sidewalk produce stand.

"Madison?"

Madison quickly glanced up. She pressed her hand to her chest and for a moment she forgot to breathe, she was so startled at seeing Stone. "Stone, what are you doing here?" she asked, amazed at how good he looked. It hadn't been quite two weeks since she had seen him last; twelve days exactly if you were counting and she had been unable not to do so. Seeing him reminded her how wrapped up in him she had gotten and how quickly. He was casually dressed in a pair of khaki pants and a polo shirt and she was hard pressed not to let her gaze travel the full length of him.

He was looking at her with an intensity that made her flesh tingle and a shiver moved down her spine. "You said you would stay at Uncle Corey's until I returned," he said, in a deep, husky voice that only added to her dilemma.

She licked her lips nervously and, when she remembered all the things that the reporter had said, she immediately decided that she didn't owe him an explanation, just like he didn't owe her one. "I decided to return home since Mom was okay," she said, as she went back to studying the fruit.

"I think we need to talk," he said and she looked back at him and wished she hadn't. She studied his features. There was a stubble of beard that darkened his chin and tired lines were etched under his eyes. He looked downright exhausted.

"When was the last time you had a good night's sleep?" she asked, as she continued to stare at him for a long moment. She wondered if his lack of sleep was due to all the partying he had done while in New York.

He shrugged. "Not since trying to get back to you. I was too wired up to sleep on the plane from New York to Montana and then when I arrived at Uncle Corey's and found you'd gone, I immediately left again and flew here."

She lifted an arched brow. "Why?"

"Because I have to talk to you."

She sighed. "Where are your things?"

"I checked into a hotel." He glanced around. "Is there someplace we can go and talk?"

Madison swallowed immediately. She had a feeling she knew what he had to say and thought that the last place she wanted him was in her home where she would always have memories of him being there. But it was the closest place and the least she could do was offer him a cup of coffee. "Yes, my condo is not far from here if you'd like to go there."

"Sure."

They walked side by side on the brick streets with little or no conversation between them. Occasionally, she would point out a historical landmark or some other note of interest. Moments later when she stopped in front of the elegant Ritz-Carlton Towers he met her gaze. "I live in the

Residences, a portion of the tower that has private condos," she said, after saying hello to the doorman. "The entrance is through a private lobby that is separate from the hotel."

He nodded as he followed her inside to the lavishly styled lobby that led to a private elevator. "How long have you lived here?" he asked as they stepped onto the elevator.

"Ever since I finished college at twenty-one. My father left me a trust fund and I decided to invest a part of it in a place that I knew would increase in value. It's located within walking distance from my job and I like the ultimate amenity of having the hotel as an extension of my home. We use the same hotel staff and any packages, dry cleaning and other deliveries I get are held until I get home. I have access to all the restaurants in the hotel, as well as all the hotel's facilities like their spa and pool." She smiled. "And on those days that I come home too tired to cook, I can even order room service."

Stone liked what he saw the moment he walked into her condo. It was spacious and elegantly decorated. He could tell the furniture was expensive and added soothing warmth to the interior of the room. "I have one bedroom, one and a half baths, a living room with a fireplace, a kitchen and a library, and it's just the size I need," she said, crossing the room to open the blinds. The floor-to-ceiling window provided a breathtaking view of Boston.

His attention was drawn to the beautiful white piano in the middle of her living room. She saw where his gaze had gone and said, "That was the last Christmas gift my father gave me before he died. And for me, at fifteen, it was like a dream come true. Sauter pianos are renowned for their outstanding sound, fine touch and unique expressiveness." She brushed some curls back from her face and added, "And as you can also see, it's pleasing to the eye. There's not a day that goes by that I don't admire it whenever I look at it. It's brought me hours of joy."

He nodded. "Do you play it often?"

"Yes. Playing the piano relaxes me." She decided not to tell him that when she had returned from Montana two days ago, it had been the sound of the music she had played on her piano that had brought solace to her aching heart. "If you'd like to have a seat, I'll fix us a cup of coffee."

"Thanks, I'd appreciate it." He watched her leave the room. He had played out in his mind what he was going to say to her and now that the time had come for him to say it, he wondered if he would have trouble getting the words out. He was a master at putting words down on paper but now that it was a matter of the heart, he was at a loss for words. He needed to let her know just how much he loved her and how much she meant to him and that, more than anything, he wanted her in his life. Loving her was more than a stone cold surrender. It was a lifeline he needed to make his life complete.

He sat down on the sofa, liking the softness of the leather. The entire room had her scent and he was engulfed in the pleasantly sweet fragrance of her. He leaned his head back and decided to close his eyes for a second. He could hear her moving around in the kitchen and in the distance he could hear the sound of boats tooting their horns as they passed in the harbor and the faint sound of an airplane that flew overhead. But his mind tuned out everything as he slowly drifted into a deep sleep.

* * *

"I forgot to ask how you want your—"

Madison stopped talking in midsentence when she saw that Stone had literally passed out on her sofa. Quickly walking over to the linen closet she pulled out a blanket and crossed the room back to him. She touched his shoulder. "Stone, you're tired," she said softly. "Go ahead and stretch out on my sofa and rest for a moment."

Glazed, tired eyes stared at her. "But we need to talk, Madison," he said in a voice that was heavy with sleep and weighty with exhaustion.

"And we *will* talk," she said softly, quietly. "As soon as you wake up from your nap. Okay?"

He nodded as he stretched out on her sofa. She placed the blanket over him and moments later his even breathing filled the room. She sighed. He was intent on talking to her and she didn't want to think about what he had to say. He probably thought, considering the affair they'd shared, that he owed her the courtesy of letting her know that things were over between them and he was moving on.

She didn't want to think about it and decided to take a shower and relax and try to forget he was there until he woke up and made his presence known. But as she looked down at him she realized that, even if he didn't make a sound, she would know that Stone was within reaching distance and for her that was not good. It was not good at all.

Stone slowly opened his eyes as soft music drifted around him. He immediately recognized it as a piece by Bach. When Delaney had been around eight or nine, she had taken music lessons for a short time and he distinctly remembered that same classical number as being one she had relentlessly hammered on the piano as she prepared for her first recital. He slowly sat upright and gradually stood, folding up the blanket Madison had placed over him.

He sighed deeply. He had come all this way to talk to her and instead he had passed out on her. He stretched his muscles then decided to go look for her. He needed to let her know how he felt about her and hoped she felt the same way about him.

Stone found her standing on a balcony that extended from her bedroom. She had changed out of the slacks and silk shirt she'd been wearing to a long flowing skirt and a matching top. She was standing barefoot, leaning against the rail with a glass of wine in her hand as she looked at the city below. He was sure he'd been quiet, that he hadn't made a sound, but still she turned and looked straight at him. Their gaze held for several moments and when a small smile touched her lips, his stomach tightened in response to that smile. "How was your nap?" she asked.

He covered the distance separating them and came to stand beside her. "I didn't mean to pass out on you like that."

"You were tired."

"Yes, I guess I was."

"And you're probably hungry. I can order room ser—"

"We need to talk, Madison."

She turned back to look out over the city. "You know you really didn't have to come, Stone. I understood how things were from the beginning so you don't owe me an explanation."

Stone lifted a brow, wondering what she was talking about. "I don't?"

She turned and met his gaze. "No, you don't. You never misled me or implied that anything serious was developing between us. In fact you were very honest from the beginning in letting me know how much you enjoyed your freedom and that you never planned to marry." She inhaled deeply. "So you're free to go."

He gazed at her for a moment as if enthralled by all she had said, and then asked, "I'm free to go where?"

She shrugged. "Back to New York, Montana, on your European book tour or anywhere you want to go. I guess you figured that, with your uncle marrying my mom, we should end things between us in a proper way so there won't be any hard feelings and I just want to assure you that there won't be. No matter what, Stone, I will always consider you my friend."

Stone took the glass of wine from her hand after suddenly deciding that he was the one who needed a drink. He looked at the glass and made sure that he placed his mouth on the exact spot that showed the imprint of her lips. The white wine tasted good and felt bubbly as it flowed down his throat. He emptied the glass then set it on the table next to where they were standing. He then met Madison's curious gaze. "So you think that's the reason I'm here? To bring our intimate association to a proper close?" he asked, managing a soft smile.

She met his gaze. "Isn't it?"

Her question, asked in a quiet, soft voice, stirred something deep inside Stone and he regretted more than ever that he had never told her that he loved her. She needed to know that. She needed to know that each and every time he had made love to her had meant more to him than just satisfying overzealous hormones. Yes, he had taken her with a hunger that had almost bordered on obsession, and he had always been acutely aware of everything physical about her. But he had also been aware of her emotional side. That had been what had first touched his heart. Her love and concern for the people she cared about.

Knowing he needed to get her out of the vicinity of her bedroom, he took her hand in his. "Come on. Let's go into the living room and talk."

He led her through the bedroom and into the living room. When she started to sit beside him on the sofa, he pulled her into his arms and placed her in his lap. He smiled at the look of surprise that lit her features.

"Now then, I think I need to get a few things straight up front," he said.

She lifted a brow. "Such as?"

"The reason I'm here and the reason I hadn't gotten any sleep in over forty-eight hours. First let me start off by saying I'm not going back to New York or Montana, and I'm sure as hell not going on some European book tour—unless you go to all of those places with me."

Madison blinked, confused. "I don't understand."

Stone chuckled. "Evidently. And in a way it's entirely my fault. I failed to make something clear to you each time that we made love."

He saw how her throat tightened when she swallowed. "What?"

He met her gaze and held on to it, locked it with his. "That I love you."

She pulled back and stared at him in disbelief. "But, but, I—I didn't know," she said, her words coming out in a stream of astonished puffs of air.

He skimmed a fingertip across her lips. "That's why I'm here, Madison, to let you know. I think I fell in love with you the moment I saw you on the airplane, although it took me a while to come to terms with it. I should have told you before I left for New York, but I was in a rush to leave and decided to wait and tell you when I got back. The trip took longer than I expected. I watched that television show, just as you did, but I didn't think when you heard what the reporter said that you would believe it had anything to do with my relationship with you. When she interviewed me I didn't want to mention you or tell her how I felt about you, mainly because I wanted to keep things between us private. Besides, I wasn't sure how you felt about me since we hadn't talked."

He leaned over and replaced his fingers with his lips and brushed a kiss across her mouth. "And I still don't know. I've told you how I feel about you, but you've yet to say how you feel about me."

Madison snuggled closer into Stone's arms and reached up and placed her arms around his neck. The same happiness that shone in her heart was reflected in her eyes. "I love you, Stone Westmoreland, with all my heart. I think I fell in love with you the first moment I looked into your eyes on the airplane, too. And I was so embarrassed when I realized where my hand had been and how close I came to touching a certain part of you. But now I know it went there for a reason," she said, shifting her body and reaching down to actually touch him.

She smiled upon realizing how hard he was and what that meant. "I didn't know at the time that that part of you, all of you, was destined to be mine and I feel like the luckiest and the happiest woman in the world."

Stone groaned out her name as he captured her mouth and deepened the kiss when she sank into him, returning his kiss the way he had taught her to do, enjoying the passion that would always be there between them. Moments later he pulled back and cupped her face in his hands.

"Will you marry me, Madison? Will you agree to spend the rest of your life with me and be my soul mate? I know how much you love Boston and that you don't ever want to leave and that's fine. We can make our primary home here and—"

Madison quickly touched her mouth to his to cut off his words. "Yes, I'll marry you, Stone. I love you and my home will always be wherever you are. I know how much you like to travel and now, after visiting Montana and seeing so much beauty there, I see what I've been missing by not traveling. Now I want to go to those places with you."

Her words touched him and he reached out, pulled her back into his arms and again kissed her, long and deep. When he lifted his head, he stood up with her in his arms. "I love you," he told her again as he carried her into the bedroom. He gently placed her on the bed and stood back. He then reached into his pocket and pulled out a small white velvet box.

"I bought this for you while in New York. I had every intention of asking you to marry me when I got back to Montana." He leaned forward and handed her the box.

With tears misting her eyes, Madison nervously opened it to find a beautiful diamond engagement ring. It was so lovely that it took her breath away. She gazed back at Stone. "I—I don't know what to say."

Stone chuckled. "Baby, you've already said everything I

wanted to hear. The only thing left is for us to set the date. I don't want to seem like I'm rushing things, but I want us to get married as soon as possible…. I'll understand if you prefer to wait until next June and have a huge wedding here."

Madison shook her head. "No, I had planned a big wedding with Cedric and I don't want that for us. We don't need it. We can go before the justice of the peace and I'd be happy. I just want to be your wife."

Stone's smile widened. "And more than anything, I want to be your husband. Before leaving Montana, Uncle Corey suggested the Westmorelands get-together at his place the second week in August. He wants everyone to meet Abby, as well as his sons and daughter. I know that's only six weeks from now but what do you think of us having a wedding then, there on Corey's mountain?" he asked, taking the ring and placing it on her finger. He liked the way it looked. He could tell that she liked the way it looked, too. She held her hand out in front of her and kept peeking at it, smiling.

She then glanced up at him. "I think August will be a wonderful time. When do you leave for Europe?"

He shook his head. "I haven't agreed to that book tour, Madison. Everything hinges on what you want to do. I know how much you like teaching and—"

She leaned up and placed a finger to his lips. "Yes, I've always enjoyed teaching because that's what I limited myself to do. I appreciated those nights when you came into my bedroom at Corey's and shared your writing with me. And, because of it, I now have a burning desire to do something I've always wanted to do but was never brave enough to try."

"What?"

A wishful thought flashed across her face. "Compose my own music. I once shared a few pieces I'd composed with a friend at school and she told me how good she thought they were and that it was something I should do. And I think I will."

He pulled her into his arms. "I think that's a wonderful idea and is one that I wholeheartedly support." He nuzzled her neck, liking her scent and thinking he would never get enough of it.

Madison looped her arms around his neck and pulled him down on the bed with her and he kissed her slowly, deeply and began removing her clothes. When he had her completely naked, he sat back on his haunches and stared at her, a deep look of love in his eyes.

"It's your turn, Stone. Take off your clothes," she said softly, pulling at his shirt.

He stood, appearing more than happy to oblige. She watched as he removed every stitch of clothing and, when he rejoined her on the bed, she reached out and ran her finger down his chest. "This is nice," she said, leaning forward and flicking her tongue across his hardened nipples.

When she felt his shudder, Madison felt confident, loved and, thanks to Stone, passionate. She moved her hand lower and let her fingers travel past his waist and stroke that part of him she had almost touched on the plane. She heard his breathing increase and felt his body harden even more beneath her hand. He also felt hot and ready.

"You want me," she said softly, marveling at how much he did.

"Yes, and I'll always want you." He gently pushed her

back on the bed to touch her everywhere, kiss her everywhere, taste her everywhere; and when she couldn't take any more and was thrashing about beneath him, he covered her mouth with his the same moment that he parted her legs, lifted her hips and eased inside of her. She shifted her body to welcome him and, with one quick thrust, he was bedded deep inside her.

He held himself still in that position as his mouth mated relentlessly with hers, filled with emotions of every kind. And when her muscles began clenching his heated flesh, he slowly began moving, establishing a rhythm that would bring them both pleasure.

Moments later when they both went spiraling off the edge, lost in passion of the richest kind, Stone knew his parents' prediction of love at first sight had been right. Loving Madison was something he would look forward to doing for the rest of his life.

Epilogue

When Stone and Madison returned to Montana they discovered that Corey and Abby had decided not to wait for a Christmas wedding but wanted to marry sooner. So the four of them—Corey, Abby, Stone and Madison—decided to have a double wedding on Corey's Mountain in August. Martin Quinn, a former judge, agreed to perform the ceremony.

Now the day of the wedding had arrived and, as Madison glanced around, she knew that only Abby Winters-Westmoreland could bring such style, grace and elegance to the rugged mountains of Montana for the mother-and-daughter wedding. Almost everyone had arrived by plane on the airstrip that several ranchers in the area shared. Her mother had even had a band flown in for the affair, as well as a well-known catering company from Boston. Every time she glanced over at her mother and Corey she saw just how happy they were together. It had taken thirty-two years but they were finally together and she knew it was meant to be this way.

"Ready?"

Madison glanced up at her husband of less than an hour and knew it was time to meet the rest of his siblings and cousins. She had met his parents, his sister Delaney, her husband Prince Jamal Ari Yasir and their son Ari last night. Almost everyone else had arrived an hour or two before the wedding was to take place, so she hadn't had the chance to meet them beforehand.

"Yes, I'm ready," she said, inhaling deeply.

Stone leaned down and kissed her lips; then, taking her hand in his, he led her over to an area where a group stood talking. A couple of people she recognized, but others she did not.

First he introduced her to his married brothers, Dare and Thorn, and their wives, Shelly and Tara. Madison could immediately feel the love flowing between the couples and hoped that her and Stone's marriage would be just as strong and loving.

Stone then introduced her to his brother, the one he said the ladies called "The Perfect Storm." She could see why. He was drop-dead gorgeous and she had a strong feeling that he knew it. Then she met Storm's fraternal twin, Chase, and he was just as gorgeous. In fact she was discovering that all the male Westmorelands were good-looking men.

Next came the cousins: Jared, Spencer, Ian, Quade and Reggie. She had already met Quade and Durango, and

Durango pulled her into his arms and gave her an as-
tounding, welcome-to-the-family kiss on her lips and said
he liked her even if she was a city girl. She gave Stone a
questioning look and the response in his eyes indicated
that he would explain things later.

She then got the chance to see the newest Westmoreland
cousins again; Clint and Cole, as well as the daughter
Corey Westmoreland never knew he had: Casey.

Casey Westmoreland was shockingly beautiful and
Madison thought it amusing to see how all the single men
present who weren't Westmorelands were giving her their
undivided attention. Now she understood what Clint and
Cole had meant when they'd insinuated that it hadn't been
easy being Casey's brothers.

After all the introductions were made, Stone pulled
Madison into his arms. They would be leaving the mountain in a few hours to spend a week in San Francisco. Her
mother and Corey were headed in the opposite direction
to spend a week in Jamaica.

Madison had never been to the Bay area and Stone,
who'd been there several times, had planned a special hon-
eymoon there for them.

They would be leaving the country within the month for
Stone's four-month European book tour. They would re-
turn just weeks before Christmas and had decided to make
Atlanta their primary home.

"I can't wait to get you all to myself," Stone whispered
to his wife moments later, when her mother had indicated
it was time to cut the cake and to take more pictures.

"I can't wait to get you all to myself, too," Madison said

smiling and meaning every word. She had a surprise for him. She had composed a song just for him. And she knew as she gazed lovingly at her husband that it was a song that would stay in her heart forever.

* * * * *